DAVIN

DAVIN

DAN GORDON AND
ZAKI GORDON

DELACORTE PRESS

Published by
Delacorte Press
Bantam Doubleday Dell Publishing Group, Inc.
1540 Broadway
New York, New York 10036

Library of Congress Cataloging-in-Publication Data

Gordon, Dan (Daniel).
Davin / Dan Gordon and Zaki Gordon.
p.   cm.
Summary: As a child lies ill with fever, the figures of a bugle boy, a blustery sergeant major, a princess, and other toys come to life and search for the mysterious Davin, a powerful figure who can cure the boy.
ISBN 0-385-32221-6 (alk. paper)
[1. Toys—Fiction.   2. Fantasy.]   I. Gordon, Zaki.   II. Title.
PZ7.G6545Dav   1997
[Fic]—dc20   96-31835
                                                                          CIP
                                                                           AC

The text of this book is set in 13-point Adobe Garamond.
Book design by Susan Clark
Manufactured in the United States of America
April 1997
BVG   10   9   8   7   6   5   4   3   2   1

This book is for Grandma Goddess. She was the mother of one of the authors and the grandmother of the other. She was the best storyteller and the best friend any child could have. This book is the first of what the authors hope will be a long line of Grandma Goddess stories. She had a lot of them.

Introduction

This story, like all stories, is magic. How you read it depends on whether you're a kid or a grown-up. If you're a kid, you ought to have this book read *to* you, just the way we did. It can be read to you by your grandma or grandpa, by your mom or dad, by your aunt or uncle, possibly even by your big brother or big sister, or by anyone significantly older than you who loves you. That is very important. It will make the story better.

This story sounds best when you are in bed with jammies on. If you don't have jammies you can wear a nightshirt, but it should be something warm and snuggly, very soft and comfortable, and it should smell like you.

If you think you are too old to call pajamas jammies, you have a bad attitude and you have begun to stifle your imagination. Unstifle it! Jammies are the things you wear when you're warm and comfortable in bed and the world is fine and nothing can hurt you. It's that way whether you're seven or forty-eight. Grandma Goddess lived to be eighty-three and she still believed in jammies, so there.

In addition to jammies, you should have your favorite blanket, quilt or comforter. If you don't have one, you should get one. You should have a comfortable pillow, maybe two. The kind you can squish up. And you should have, when it is called for in the story, hot chocolate. You can have it in a cup or a mug, it's up to you. We think it ought to have a marshmallow floating on top, but there are some people who don't like marshmallows—they like whipped cream. That's up to you, too. But you should definitely have hot chocolate. Unless you like tea. Tea is an acceptable hot drink in this story.

So let's say in this story that you're at the point where the grandma is reading to her grandchildren and the grandchildren take a noisy sip from their hot chocolates and then smack their lips and say, "Ahhhh."

What do you think you should do? Sit there like a latke? Like a bump on a log, like a wart on a frog? Hmmmm?

You should do exactly what the kids in the story do. When they take a noisy sip, you should take a noisy sip. When the kids smack their lips, you smack yours. You know why you should do exactly what the kids in the story do? Because you *are* a kid in the story.

Now, if you're *not* a kid and if you are in fact the big person who is reading this aloud, you may read the story to your grandson or granddaughter, son or daughter, niece or nephew, little brother, little sister or child you are baby-sitting, but you must, if this thing is to work as it should, read it to a child you love. That way you will not feel like a fool doing the sound effects and all the voices and accents, noises, snorts, snuffs, sniffles, harrumphs and hachoos you may be called upon to perform.

This is going to be the most fun you've had all day, and you will remember this the rest of your life, long after the child who looks at you now with sleepy eyes wide, full of expectation, has grown to be taller and stronger than you. You will both remember this time. . . .

◆ ◆ ◆ ◆ ◆ 1 ◆ ◆ ◆ ◆ ◆

Grandma Goddess

G randma Goddess was coming for the weekend. For Yoni and Adam and their cousin Danielle, who was staying with them for two weeks that summer, that meant there would be treats from Grandma Goddess's purse. Grandma Goddess never came without treats. They were little things, little teeny tiny treasures of the kind that only grandmas notice and get for their grandchildren. There might be a toy horse for Danielle's collection, an action figure for Yoni to have adventures with, and for Adam there were always strange things because, well . . . Adam was strange.

He was four years old. Yoni was eight and Danielle, their cousin, was almost ten. One night when Adam's mother and father were putting him to bed, they gave him a big steaming cup of hot chocolate as a special treat, even though they knew he would be up before long going to the bathroom. He blew on the hot chocolate three times to cool it off and then took a big noisy slurpy sip.★

He blew on the hot chocolate three times to cool it off and then took a big noisy slurpy sip. Then he smacked his lips and said, "Ahhhh," quite contentedly.

Then as his mother and father were kissing him good night and saying Good night, sleep tight, don't let the bedbugs bite, Adam said, "There aren't any bedbugs on Mars."

Adam's father looked at Adam's mother and Adam's mother looked at Adam's father and then they both looked at Adam.

"What do you mean?" asked Adam's father.

"About what?" said Adam innocently.

"What do you mean, there aren't any bedbugs on Mars?"

"Well," said Adam quite reasonably, "there aren't."

"But what does that have to do with you and with us saying good night to you?" asked Adam's mother.

"Well," said Adam, "that's where I live."

"Where?" said his father.

"On Mars," Adam said. And then he explained. "Every

★ *Authors' Note*
As we said in the introduction, this is your cue. "He blew on the hot chocolate three times to cool it off and then took a big noisy slurpy sip." In other words, now would be a great time for you to blow on *your* hot chocolate and slurpily sip same. Just a suggestion, mind you . . . no one is trying to say what your interaction with this book ought to be. It's just that if *I* had a cup of hot chocolate, now would be a good time to blow.

night after you kiss me good night and turn out the lights, 7
I go up to Mars."

"Uh-huh," said Adam's father. "And how do you get
there?"

"In my bed," said Adam, as if his father were foolish to
even ask.

"And what do you do there?" Adam's mother asked.

"I have a job," said Adam very proudly.

"Really," said his mother. "What's your job?"

"I lock up," Adam said. "I have a key and I lock up."

Adam's mother and father laughed. They told the story
many times to many people and all of them laughed, too.
Adam didn't care for that at all.

It seemed to him that they were making fun of him and
his job and his key. But when Grandma Goddess came
for a visit shortly thereafter, she didn't laugh. Besides, she
had a present.

"What is it?" Adam said.

"Open it up and you'll see," said Grandma Goddess.

Adam tore open the wrapping paper and found a little
box. He opened the box and found a piece of cotton. He
pulled up the piece of cotton and found a keychain. Attached to the keychain was a little tag. It was leatherette or
maybe even plastic and it had white words printed on it.

"What's it say?" asked Adam excitedly.

"It says," said Grandma Goddess, putting her arm
around him and sitting next to him on his bed, " 'Key to
Mars.' "

Adam looked at Grandma Goddess and said, "Cool."

There were two other things that Yoni and Adam and Danielle looked forward to every time Grandma Goddess came to visit. Pinch cookies and stories.

Pinch cookies were made of dough and had chocolate chips in them and you rolled the dough into balls and then pinched it between your fingers until it looked like a Hershey's kiss and then you baked them and they were better than anything.

Stories were what Grandma Goddess read at bedtime.

Bedtime stories with Grandma Goddess could not begin until you were in jammies, in your bed with your favorite blankie, a steaming cup of hot chocolate with a marshmallow floating on top and, possibly, a pinch cookie or two.

Danielle's favorite blanket was her dribble blanket because it had things she called dribbles sewn into it that you could stick between your toes and they felt good in bed at night as you were falling asleep. It was a baby blanket but she loved it long after she had grown into a little girl. At home she tucked it under her comforter and she always brought it with her when she slept at her cousins' house.

Yoni had his blankie, which he sometimes held around his neck like a cape pretending to be a superhero. Adam had his Dallas Cowboys blanket but more important to him by far was his key to Mars, which he slept with every night.

All three children had their hot chocolate in their special mugs. Adam had his happy as a clam mug. It was green and there was a smiling clam in the bottom that you could see only after you had drunk everything inside. Danielle had her pony mug. It was bright yellow and it had horses. And Yoni had his monster mug. It had a monster. There were four pinch cookies on a plate, one for each of them and one for Grandma Goddess.

"What are you gonna read, Grandma Goddess?" Adam asked impatiently.

"Hold on there, boy," Grandma Goddess said as she lowered herself into one of the tiny chairs in Adam's room. "Criminitly."

Criminitly was something Grandma Goddess said in the same way that other people would say Geeminee Christmas. No one ever knew what it meant.

Grandma Goddess didn't even know what it meant, nor did Yoni, nor did Adam's father, who was, after all, Grandma Goddess's son.

The closest they could all figure out was that "Criminitly" was really "Crime in Italy," though why it should matter to Grandma Goddess that there was crime in Italy and why she should want to share that concern with her grandchildren was anyone's guess. To the best of anyone's knowledge, Grandma Goddess had never been to Italy and the only Italian food she liked was pizza and spaghetti. It was just something she said and it seemed to make sense.

"Criminitly," Grandma Goddess said, "I'm an old lady, just let me sit down."

She pulled out a book that none of them had ever seen before. It looked old and worn and it was called *Davin— The Secrets of the Bear.*

Grandma Goddess opened the book as if she were about to read and then she looked up and her voice went very soft and very low.

"I don't know," she said, "if I should read this to you or not. It could be . . . scary."

"It's not gonna be scary, Grandma Goddess," said Adam. He took another noisy sip from his hot chocolate and then looked up at her with a frightened expression in his eyes and said, "Is it?"

"I have an idea," Yoni said. "Let's turn out some lights."

And so they did. They turned out the lamp on the bookshelf and it got darker. They turned off the lamp that sat in the corner and it got darker still. Then Grandma Goddess moved in closer toward the lamp on the night table near Adam's bed. She opened the book and began to read . . .

◆ ◆ ◆ ◆ 2 ◆ ◆ ◆ ◆

The Ultimate Battle Between the Forces of Good and Evil

"I have to go to the bathroom," Adam said.

"Criminitly," said Yoni, annoyed with his little brother.

The Ultimate Battle Between the Forces of Good and Evil—Part II

"**D**oes anyone else have to go to the bathroom?" asked Grandma Goddess.

"No," said Adam, "I just went."

"No," said Danielle, "I don't have to."

"Come on, Grandma," said Yoni, "start the story."

"All right," said Grandma Goddess, "if you promise not to be afraid."

And she began to read.

"Picture in your mind a gargoyle . . ."

"A gargle?" asked Danielle.

"Not a gargle," said Grandma Goddess, and her voice got low and sort of scary, like the voice in the haunted house at Disneyland when it says Have you noticed there are no doors, no windows here . . . No way out . . .

"Not a gargle," said Grandma Goddess, and her voice got low and sort of scary, almost like a ghost's. "A gargle is a mouthwash . . . it's something you do in the back of your throat with medicine or salt water. No, no . . . this is a gargoyle, a stone monster."

"Yeah, a gargoyle, not a gargle," said Yoni, although in truth he had not known what a gargoyle was himself until Grandma Goddess had explained it.

Poor Danielle felt a little embarrassed at not knowing her gargles from her gargoyles, but Adam took her hand and said reassuringly, "We call them gargles on Mars, too."

"But in this story," Grandma Goddess said, "we call it a gargoyle. A monster carved in granite, half bird, half demon, with a horrible, frightening, snarling face, and giant claws that grip the brickwork of the building on which it sits. You can see these carved stone monsters on buildings throughout Europe. They put them there for decoration or perhaps to scare off evil things. This particular gargoyle sits on top of a building. Can you see it? Can you see it in your mind's eye?

"A carved stone figure sitting on its haunches, its claws digging into the brick building on which it is perched. But surely there's nothing to be afraid of. It's made of stone, after all . . . Certainly there's no reason to be frightened of this thing because it's not alive, after all, is it?"

Grandma Goddess leaned in toward them and her shadow danced on the wall behind her. "Is it?" she said again.

"Look closely, more closely still. . . . There in the

dark its eyes are starting to glow. Dimly at first, a pinkish glow burns brighter and then red-hot. And look at its claws: Could it be that they're beginning to clutch the bricks more tightly? Does the red brick dust crumble beneath the claws, tightening like a vise as the monster sits up ever so slightly on its haunches and stares down at you with those red, glowing eyes?"

Grandma Goddess looked from one to the other and leaned back and said in her normal voice, "You're sure this isn't too scary?"

No one said a word and so Grandma Goddess continued.

"Now picture something else," she said. "Hills in the early-morning light. You can see them . . . in this misty light of blue dawn, they look almost as fuzzy and blue as a child's blanket. Now listen . . . What do you hear? The sounds of an army marching . . . the clump clump clump of feet marching," said Grandma Goddess, and she clump-clump-clumped with her feet upon the floor, and the children could hear it in their minds, could hear the army marching.

"Listen harder," she said. "There are drums drumming as the army marches. Fuh-da-dum . . . Fuh-da-dum . . . Fuh-da-dum-dum-dum . . . Fuh-da-dum . . . Fuh-da-dum . . . Fuh-da-dum-dum-dum . . .

"The army is getting closer. And now you can hear wagons creaking and the sounds of horses' hooves and wagon drivers saying Giddyup there! And the sounds of leather harness and the wagon wheels and the squeaky springs and creaky sounds of wooden yokes and iron wheels with wooden spokes as the drums keep drumming, the feet keep marching and the army draws closer, ever closer, coming around from behind the mountains and the hills that look so fuzzy in the blue light of dawn. And now if you listen harder, there are other sounds. Metal clanking against metal, almost like the sound of armor, of swords in scabbards clanging against suits of armor on knights who ride on mighty steeds that snort and stamp their feet and strain against the reins held by the mighty men of war dressed in suits of shining armor."

"Wait a second," said Yoni indignantly. "What kind of army is this?"

"What do you mean?" asked Danielle.

"You can't have all these guys in the same army," Yoni tried to explain.

"Sure you can," said Danielle. "You can have whatever sort of army you want in a story."

Because Danielle was a girl, Yoni did not expect her to pick up on the finer points of armies, so he turned to Grandma Goddess, whom he considered a bit more enlightened on the subject, and asked for an explanation. "Grandma, what kind of army is this with drums and horses and marching guys and knights in armor?"

"You'll see," said Grandma Goddess. "You'll see," she said again, and then mumbled to herself, "Now . . . where was I . . ."

She looked down at the book, trying to find her place, said, "Criminitly," and then continued.

". . . held by mighty men of war dressed in suits of shining armor. Then they came around from behind the hill and you could see them. An army unlike any army that anyone had ever seen before. There were World War One infantry soldiers with tin hats, long rifles with fixed bayonets, gas masks and canteens that clanked against their bodies, and there were Queen's Own Cavalry in shining silver breastplates on splendid horses with glorious plumes sticking up and blowing in the breeze from shining helmets and leather harness. There were cowboys dressed in chaps and ten-gallon hats and Indians with full eagle-feather warbonnets and beaded moccasins and leather fringes riding bareback with lances, bows and arrows.

"There were Knights of the Round Table with squires who marched before them carrying their shields and all of them were led by a British regimental colonel in full dress uniform. And behind him marched his blustery sergeant major with a huge handlebar mustache, and next to him there was a little Union Army bugle boy from the American Civil War."

"Grandma Goddess," said Yoni in an exasperated tone of voice, "this is crazy! This is nuts! Knights and World War One guys and cowboys and Indians and this little bugle boy? And all these guys make up one army?"

"Yes," said Grandma Goddess. "In fact," she said, "the Bugle Boy looks just like Adam here, and Danielle looks just like Princess Helen."

"Who's Princess Helen?" asked Danielle.

"Princess Helen," said Grandma Goddess, "is the one they're all going to rescue, for she has been taken prisoner by the horrible Dark Knight. He has kidnapped her and is holding her to learn the whereabouts of the great Davin. Princess Helen knows part of the secret of where he is, and without Davin all of them," said Grandma Goddess, "all of the Cowboys and the Indians, all of the Knights and Queen's Own Cavalry, the Regimental Colonel with the full white beard and the Blustery Sergeant Major with the big mustache, the Civil War Bugle Boy, Princess Helen and the Dark Knight, in fact, their entire world and all who are in it will perish without Davin . . ."

◆ ◆ ◆ ◆ 4 ◆ ◆ ◆ ◆

The Army of
the Dark Knight

"Grandma Goddess," said Yoni as he blew on his hot chocolate and took such a noisy slurp that it left a chocolate mustache on his upper lip.

"Yes," said Grandma Goddess.

"Doesn't anyone look like me?" Yoni put his nose into the hot chocolate mug once again and looked down as if he didn't care whether anyone in the story looked like him or not. "You said the Bugle Boy looked like Adam and Princess Helen looked like Danielle . . ." He let his thought trail off.

Grandma Goddess waited until he looked up. Yoni had the biggest, most beautiful eyes of the three children and she waited until those eyes were looking into hers, and then she said, "Perseus."

"Who?" said Yoni.

"The hero," said Grandma Goddess. "But you've got to wait until he comes into the story."

"Criminitly," said Yoni.

"Yes," said Grandma Goddess, "isn't that a revolting development."

"Isn't that a revolting development" was also something that Grandma Goddess had a habit of saying.

"Grandma Goddess," said Adam, "what happened to the story?"

"Nothing happened to it at all," said Grandma Goddess. "I'm about to read it."

And that's just what she did.

As the ragtag army marched out from around the hills and down into the valley, they did not know it, but they were being watched. High up above them on a cliff overlooking the valley into which they now marched stood the terrible . . . fearsome . . . evil Dark Knight. He was clad entirely in the blackest armor and a bloodred cape hung from his shoulders. Behind him and lying at his feet, tied up and gagged, was the brave and beautiful Princess Helen. She struggled against the ropes that tied her hands and ankles together but the knots were too strong, and try as she might she could not wriggle free. She watched as the Dark Knight looked down at the ragtag army made up of all her friends marching out into the valley below. The Dark Knight laughed cruelly as he thought of the ambush he was about to unleash on the soldiers who marched before him. He turned to Princess Helen. His voice was low and menacing.

"Look, Your Highness," he said, pointing down into the valley, "the fools are marching into my trap. When I give the signal my cavalry shall charge down upon them."

He stretched out his hand and Princess Helen's gaze followed the direction in which his finger pointed. On a rise just below them stood a troop of headless horsemen holding swords in one hand and reining in their horses with the other. They were a frightful sight. You've probably heard the story of Ichabod Crane and the Legend of Sleepy Hollow. Poor Ichabod only had to deal with one headless horseman, but this was an entire army of beheaded cavalry waiting to charge down into the valley.

"You're sure this isn't too scary?" asked Grandma Goddess.

The three children shook their heads, meaning no, but in fact they were too frightened to speak. Grandma Goddess put on her Dark Knight voice and continued.

"And look over there," the Dark Knight said, and his crimson cape billowed around his arm as he pointed to the opposite cliff. "Behind those rocks are hidden all my bowmen, the finest archers in the world. The very best there are."

"Robin Hood's the best there is," said Adam.

Grandma Goddess nodded in agreement and said in her Dark Knight voice, "The very best there are, except for Robin Hood. And he's a good guy, so he won't have anything to do with me. But even without Robin Hood, my bowmen and my headless cavalrymen will make quick work of your foolish friends. Mahahahahaha . . . ," he

laughed cruelly. "Hahahahahaha . . . ," he laughed
again.

"Why is he laughing so much, Grandma?" Adam asked.

"Because," said Grandma Goddess, "he's a happy bad guy."

"Shhh," said Yoni, shushing his little brother. "Go ahead, Grandma, the bad guys are up there, the good guys are in the valley . . ."

"I don't know," said Grandma Goddess, "you look tired to me. Maybe we should stop for the night."

"No," said Yoni, "we're not tired."

"We're not tired at all," said Danielle.

"It's still early on Mars, Grandma," Adam said.

"All right," said Grandma Goddess, "just a little while more."

"Someone has to warn them," Princess Helen thought. And she moved her head back and forth, trying to wiggle the gag out of her mouth, and loosened it just enough to shout out a warning. "Watch out!" she yelled. "It's a trap!"

Her words echoed off every hillside. "It's a trap-rap-rap-rap . . . ," her voice echoed through the valley.

"A trap?" said the Regimental Colonel. "I say, did someone say, 'Watch out, it's a trap'?"

The Dark Knight was furious as he watched the Regimental Colonel bark out orders to move his army into a defensive position.

"You fool," the Dark Knight said to Princess Helen,

"you think you can stop me?" He raised his hand as high as he could stretch it and signaled to the bowmen, who let fly a volley of arrows from their hiding places in the rocks up above.

Flaming arrows rained down upon the ragtag army and the soldiers looked up in terror as the troop of headless cavalrymen charged down upon them, streaming down the hillside. The battle was fierce, with Headless Horsemen charging their steeds into the midst of the ragtag band of warriors who had come to rescue Princess Helen. The Little Bugle Boy and the Blustery Sergeant Major huddled together.

"We have to do something!" cried the Bugle Boy.

"There's nothing we can do, you little scamp," harrumphed the Blustery Sergeant Major, his knees knocking together from fright. Because the truth was, even if there had been something they could do, the Sergeant Major wouldn't have done it. He was afraid of his own shadow, let alone an army of headless cavalrymen.

"But, but, we've got to do something," said the Little Bugle Boy. "We've got to save the Princess and fight the forces of evil. We've got to!"

"The only but we've got to do," said the cowardly Sergeant Major, "is butt out! Keep our heads down, our powder dry and our noses to the grindstone. Ahem . . . ahem . . . a good soldier knows when a cause is lost and I'm afraid that's exactly the situation in which we find ourselves. Only the gods can save us now."

And as he said those very words, that only the gods

could save them now, the earth began to tremble, to shake and quake and rumble and roll in a gigantic earthquake. Hills crashed. Huge boulders broke from the mountains and fell upon the Dark Knight's army. Mountains tumbled one upon the other and giant landslides cascaded down, blocking the path of the Headless Horsemen and burying the Dark Knight's bowmen.

The Little Bugle Boy looked up and saw what was happening and picked up the flag of the ragtag army and shouted out for all around him to hear, "Charge! For Princess Helen and for Davin!"

One by one, each of the soldiers who looked up and saw the little boy leading the attack took heart and followed after the Little Bugle Boy in a ferocious charge against the Dark Knight's men.

The Headless Horsemen fell back in terror. The archers dropped their bows and ran. Even the cowardly Sergeant Major joined in the charge once he saw that the enemy was fleeing.

"After them, lads!" he shouted. "Don't let them get away!"

There was no question now that they would be victorious and rescue Princess Helen, when suddenly there was heard the sound of a door opening and of footsteps approaching. Clump clump clump clump clump . . . the sounds of sensible high-topped shoes tramped across a wooden floor and a British nanny's voice said in a high-pitched scolding tone, "Heowwwwww many times," said the voice of the Nanny, "heowwwww many times have I told you not to play with those stupid filthy toys in your sickbed?"

In a blinding flash of light, all the warriors, good and bad, froze where they were and turned into children's toys: tin soldiers, wooden and plastic figures with tiny swords and rifles frozen in their hands, and the great battlefield became the folds of a blue blanket on a little boy's trundle bed.

Then Grandma Goddess looked up from the book, closed it softly in her lap and said good night.

"Good night?" said Adam.

"Grandma Goddess!" exclaimed Danielle.

"You can't just stop there, Grandma!" said Yoni.

"Of course I can," said Grandma Goddess, and she kissed each of their foreheads, sent them in to brush their teeth, tucked them each into bed, kissed them once again and turned out the light.

5

The Nanny

All the next day Yoni and Adam and Danielle tried to get Grandma Goddess to read the next chapter.

"But it's a bedtime story," said Grandma Goddess.

"It doesn't *have* to be," said Yoni.

"It doesn't have to be, but it is," Grandma Goddess said.

"It's bedtime on M—" Adam started to say.

"I know it's bedtime on Mars," Grandma Goddess said, "but we're not on Mars."

"*He* is," Yoni said about his little brother.

"Then read us a daytime story," said Danielle sensibly.

But nothing they could do or say made any difference. As far as Grandma Goddess was concerned, this was a bedtime story and bedtime stories were read at bedtime. So they baked cookies instead. That way they would have something to eat while they listened to the story.

Later they played Monopoly and Clue, and card games like War and Spite & Malice. Grandma Goddess was good at card games.

Finally it was nighttime. After dinner the children began yawning even though it was a weekend and they were allowed to stay up later than their usual bedtime.

"I'm tired," Yoni said, yawning.

"I am, too. I'm sooo tired," said Danielle, stretching her arms out and covering her mouth as she yawned even bigger than Yoni.

Adam looked at the two of them as though they were crazy. "I'm not tired. It's not even eight o'clock. You guys are—"

But then Yoni poked him in the ribs. "We're *all* tired and we want to go to bed, understand?"

Adam looked at him as if he didn't understand at all. "I'm *not* tired," he said. And then he remembered what they had planned before dinner and looked at Grandma and said, "Oh, yes I am. I'm very tired. I'm going to sleep now. It's time for a story, Grandma."

Grandma Goddess was sitting on the sofa and Adam took her hand and started pulling her up. They made hot chocolate and brought in their plate of pinch cookies, they got into their jammies and got their favorite blankies, squished up their pillows, slurped their hot drinks, smacked their lips out loud and said, "Ahhhh." And then they were ready.

Grandma Goddess put on her reading glasses and opened the book. "Now, where was I . . ."

"All the bad guys and the good guys turned into toys," Yoni said.

"And there was a Nanny who was scolding the Little Boy," said Danielle.

"Was she a witch?" asked Adam. "How could she turn good guys and bad guys into toys?"

"She didn't turn them into toys," Yoni said, taking a slurpy sip of hot chocolate. "They were always toys. The kid in the story was just pretending. It wasn't real."

"It *was* real," Danielle insisted. "It was real in the boy's mind. He imagined the toys were real and so they were real for him."

"Right," Yoni agreed. "Like when we play with action figures."

"Oh," said Adam. "Why didn't it just say that?"

"Go ahead, Grandma," Yoni said, "read the story."

Grandma Goddess cleared her throat and began to read. "Now all of this was long ago and far away in a place called London. There was a very real war going on between the forces of good and the forces of evil. The forces of evil called themselves Nazis. They had fearsome weapons, planes and bombs, and at nighttime the Little Boy could hear the distant thud and rumble and see sometimes the nighttime sky alight with flashes, search-lights and sometimes an orange tinge glowing in the dis-tance that meant a building was on fire. The Little Boy's father was English but he had lived for many years in America, which was where the Little Boy had been born. Just before the war broke out, his father and mother moved back to the family home in London, where the Little Boy's father joined what they called the R.A.F., the Royal Air Force. He became a pilot and flew airplanes . . ."

"Whoa, cool," said Yoni.

"Way cool," said Grandma Goddess.

The Little Boy's father became for him an almost mythical figure, a warrior who flew the dark skies over London and appeared sometimes in the middle of the night to kiss his forehead and then vanish once again for weeks and weeks that seemed like forever. The Little Boy missed his father terribly, for they had always played many games of make-believe together.

The ones he liked the best were the games they played with tin soldiers and tiny toy figures that the Little Boy kept in a shoe box under his bed. They were a jumble of figures. Toy warriors of every description, some of them new and some of them old, some that belonged to the Little Boy and some that had been his father's. Some of them were broken and the Little Boy's mother suggested that they throw them out. But the Little Boy would have none of it.

"They're wounded," he said.

"And the ones without heads?" asked his mother. "I'd say they were *severely* wounded."

"Those," said the Little Boy, "are the Headless Horsemen. They're supposed to be that way."

Now, with his father gone most of the time, the Little Boy found that playing the games with the toys made him feel closer to his father, almost as if he were there. When his father couldn't come home for long periods, there would be letters with funny drawings and occasionally there would be tiny boxes tied with string that made the Little Boy's heart beat faster, for he knew that inside the box there would be a toy. It would be a little tin figure of a toy, perhaps a soldier, perhaps an American cowboy or Indian, or maybe even something like the little Civil War Bugle Boy, which his father said he bought because the Bugle Boy looked so much like the Little Boy himself.

Then the Little Boy caught the fever. That's what the grown-ups called it. At first it didn't bother him at all. He didn't mind being sick. He could stay home from school and play.

He would take the shoe box out from underneath his bed and arrange the blanket on his bed into hills and valleys, canyons and caverns, and he would put the toys behind the hills, one army here, one army there. He would set traps and ambushes. He would slay dragons and villains, and good always triumphed over evil. But this time the sickness was different.

His mother had felt his forehead and said, "He's burning up," and had called the Doctor.

The Doctor came and took his temperature and the Little Boy felt very dizzy, falling asleep and waking up, feeling cold and then hot and cold again. And he heard the Doctor say, "Yes, it's the fever."

The Doctor said he was burning up with it and the Little Boy could imagine the flames beneath his bed ready to engulf him. And that's when he thought about Davin. His father had told him about the great Davin, once. Davin had been his father's teddy bear and whenever his father had been sick when he was a little boy, he would hold tight to Davin.

"And do you know what?" his father asked.

"What?" said the Little Boy.

"Davin would whisper stories into my ear and the tighter I would hold him, the better I would feel because Davin had the power to make little boys well again and before you knew it, I'd be fit as a fiddle."

Davin had long ago disappeared into that place they call the attic. The Little Boy and his father had looked for him once, but they never found him.

Besides, the strict Nanny they hired when they moved back to London said that the child had enough toys cluttering up the place.

"I hardly think," said the Nanny, "that an asthmatic child needs some dust-filled relic on his bed."

So when the Little Boy heard the grown-ups say he was burning up, he knew he was dying and he knew only Davin could save him. He would look up from his sickbed through the skylight and see on the building across the way that horrible stone gargoyle staring down at him and in his mind he knew that the Nazis who kept his father away, and the Nanny, and the gargoyle were all to blame. Only Davin could save him now.

♦ ♦ ♦ ♦ 6 ♦ ♦ ♦ ♦

The Shoe Box

The Nanny stormed about the room going this way and that, picking up dirty laundry, socks that were inside out, shoes and trousers, a bundled-up shirt, two comic books and an empty box of candy. None of these things really mattered to the Little Boy. What *did* matter was when she started gathering up the toys, telling the boy that she had warned him what would happen.

"I warned you what would happen, didn't I, young man?" she said in her high-pitched turkeylike voice.

"Yes, Nanny, but—"

"No buts. No buts from you, my lad," she said. "I warned you what would happen if you piled your bed high with these filthy things again."

So saying, she snatched up a handful of the Queen's Own Cavalry Guards, two Indians and a Knight.

"You're a sick child, isn't that what they told you? Isn't it? Isn't it? Isn't it?" she said in her turkey gobble.

"I suppose," said the Little Boy.

"And do you know the meaning of the word 'sanitary'?" she gobbled.

The Nanny was always so sweet to his mother and so mean to him. The Little Boy's mother didn't know what the Nanny was really like.

The Little Boy looked at her and imagined a giant turkey with billowing skirts and white apron and high-topped black shoes, saying Gobble gobble gobble as she snatched up his toys.

"Sanitary," she said, hopping about the room. "It means clean, devoid of germs, not contaminated. Look at these!" she gobbled, holding up a red fist full of tin soldiers.

"Filthy," she said, "germ-laden. Disease-ridden, crawling with infectious microbes and little-boy amoebae. It's a wonder you haven't contracted the plague."

She scooped up horses and weapons, lances, bows and arrows, long rifles and tomahawks, and at each one she clicked and clucked, pursed her lips, made a gobble gobble sound and flung it into the shoe box. Then she leaned down toward the Little Boy.

"And what did I say I would do when I warned you? Hmmmm?" she said.

For the first time the Little Boy noticed whiskers growing out of her chin like pig bristles, like pictures he had seen in one of his books about warthogs. The Little Boy felt very dizzy suddenly.

"I . . . I don't remember, Nanny," he said. He felt as if the bed were spinning and he held on tight to the sheets to try to keep it still.

"The attic!" said the Nanny. "I warned you that I wouldn't have these toys cluttering up the place and making more work for poor Nanny to do, and that if they did clutter up the place and make more work for poor Nanny to do, that I would pack them off in the shoe box and trundle them up to the attic!"

"No!" exclaimed the Little Boy. "If you do that—"

"And that's just what I intend to do," said the Nanny, cutting him off. With one sweeping motion of her hand, she scooped up the rest of the toys off the Little Boy's bed, swept them to the edge and tumbled them over and into the shoe box.

"To the attic!" she cackled like the wicked witch in "Hansel and Gretel," as if she were saying Into the ovens with you.

The Little Boy was horrified.

"No, Nanny, please!" he shouted. "You can't put the Dark Knight and Princess Helen into the same box!"

The Nanny stopped. She clutched the shoe box to her bosom. She glared down at the Little Boy with the same look that the gargoyle had on the building across the way, and for an instant the Little Boy was sure that her eyes had begun to glow red.

"What did you say to me, young man?" she asked in her most menacing tone of voice.

"I said you can't put the Dark Knight and Princess Helen into the same box!" said the Little Boy miserably. He felt very ill now indeed.

"Can't?" said the Nanny. "Did these old ears of mine deceive me? Did *you* just tell *me* . . . *can't?*"

"Yes, I did," said the Little Boy, standing his ground.

The Nanny bent down until she was only an inch from his face and he saw her bloodshot little piggy eyes and pig bristle whiskers growing out her chin and smelled her awful breath, which smelled like something sour and old, like fruit peelings that were rotting.

"And why, might I ask," she whispered, "can't I?"

"Because," said the Little Boy. "If you put the Dark Knight and Princess Helen in the same box, he'll . . . he'll . . . why, he'll torture her to find out where Davin is. She knows part of the secret of where Davin is!" the Little Boy cried.

What he didn't add, what he only thought, was that Davin was the only one who could save him now.

"Nonsense," said the Nanny, spitting the word into his face. "Nonsense, that's what it is." She looked at him as if he were some strange bug under a microscope. "You're not so sick, if you ask me," she said. "If you ask me, you're not so sick at all."

She straightened herself up, made her gobble gobble sound and headed for the door, clomping along as she went. Clomp . . . clomp . . . clomp . . . clomp . . . clomp . . .

"Please, Nanny, no!" the Little Boy called after her, but she was already out the door and had shut it behind her. The Little Boy heard her slide the key into the lock and turn the lock shut, so that he could not go after her.

Inside the shoe box all was confusion and chaos. It was almost pitch-black and the only light that seeped inside the shoe box was from the little crack between the lid and the top of the cardboard. Everything was topsy-turvy as the Nanny waddled down the hall and up the stairs, carrying the shoe box under her arm.

In the confusion, the Little Bugle Boy made his way silently toward Princess Helen, whom he saw lying bound and gagged in the corner.

"Your Highness," he said, "is that you?"

"Mmmugapfgawummp," said Princess Helen.

"What did she say?" asked Danielle.

Grandma Goddess looked up from the book and over the tops of her reading glasses at Danielle, who was sitting up in her bed with her dribble blanket bundled around her.

"Mmmugapfgawummp," said Grandma Goddess.

"What does that mean?" asked Adam.

"It means she had a gag in her mouth," Yoni said with an exasperated sigh. "Go on with the story, Grandma."

"Mmmugapfgawummp," said Princess Helen.

"I say," said the Blustery Sergeant Major, who had

crawled over toward them, not so much because he wanted to help Princess Helen as, if truth be told, because he was afraid of being left alone. "What in the Devil is she saying?"

The Little Bugle Boy leaned forward and loosened Princess Helen's gag.

"Thank you," said Princess Helen, smiling. "You know you are very brave."

The Little Bugle Boy struggled to untie the knots that bound Princess Helen's hands and feet, but he could not.

"I . . . I can't untie them," he said, and his eyes started to fill up with tears of frustration.

"It doesn't matter," said Princess Helen reassuringly. "Now, listen to me. You have to get help and everything will be okay. I know part of the secret of where Davin is. He's in a cave in the shadow of the Devil."

"What does that mean?" asked the Bugle Boy.

"I haven't a clue . . . ," said Princess Helen. "You have to find El Lobo, the Spaniard. He lives somewhere in the attic. He's the oldest toy there and he's sure to know. You must continue to be brave, all right?"

But before the Little Bugle Boy could answer, he looked up and saw one of the Dark Knight's men coming toward them.

"Go quickly," whispered Princess Helen, seeing the Headless Horseman coming closer.

The brave Little Bugle Boy turned to the Blustery Sergeant Major and whispered, "Let's go!"

But the Blustery Sergeant Major was afraid. He was

afraid to go and he was afraid to stay. In fact, he was
afraid to do anything.

"But but but but," he said, like an old motorboat engine, "I don't think that we ought to—"

The Little Bugle Boy stood up and said, "Stay if you want. I'm going!"

The Blustery Sergeant Major followed along miserably as the two of them crawled up toward the crack of light that seeped in between the lid and the cardboard box. They put their hands onto the top of the box and hoisted themselves over it. Just then, the Nanny must have shifted the box in her hands because the movement made them lose their balance and they tumbled off the top of the box and fell and fell and fell and fell through the air until they landed on the hallway carpet with a thud.

The Nanny did not notice that they had fallen out behind her, and she continued her turkey waddle down the hall to the attic stairs.

The Little Bugle Boy turned to the Sergeant Major to see if he was all right. He was not all right at all. He wore the most terrified look on his face that the Little Bugle Boy had ever seen.

"What's wrong?" asked the Little Bugle Boy.

The Blustery Sergeant Major was too frightened to even speak. All he could do was point up into the air.

The Little Bugle Boy looked up to where he was pointing, straight into the very jaws of death . . . two huge

38   sets of gigantic fangs were coming down straight toward them both and a gargantuan glob of sticky goo drooled down from the dripping jaws, splattering onto the two of them in a slimy, gooey mess as the fangs opened wide and swallowed them both into total darkness.

7

Perseus

It was Aldo, the family sheepdog. He lumbered down the hall shaggy as a bear going galooomph galooomph galooomph as he flew down the short flight of stairs to the landing outside the Little Boy's room just as the Little Boy's mother was showing the Doctor inside. Aldo was big and white with gray spots and long shaggy hair that covered his eyes so that the only thing that showed was the moist black ball of his nose and his red tongue, which seemed to always be hanging out of his mouth as he made his heh-ah-heh-ah-heh-ah-heh-ah panting sounds. Aldo pushed past the Doctor. "What the dickens?" the Doctor said.

Aldo pushed past the Little Boy's mother. She threw up her hands and said, "Oh, Aldo." Then Aldo leaped up onto the Little Boy's bed.

Before the Little Boy's mother could shoo him off,

Aldo leaned down and opened his mouth and out plopped a very wet Little Bugle Boy and Blustery Sergeant Major toy onto the Little Boy's bed. They fell into a fold in the blue blanket so that no one could see them. Aldo leaned forward to the Little Boy.

"Heh-ah-heh-ah-heh-ah-heh-ah," he said, and gave the Little Boy a big wet slurping shaggy sheepdog kiss.

"Aldo, get out!" the Little Boy's mother said. "Out!" she said again, stamping her foot and pointing to the door.

Poor Aldo the sheepdog hung his head sheepishly and galooomphed down off the bed, tail between his legs, nose down toward the carpet, no longer making his happy heh-ah-heh-ah-heh-ah sounds.

Aldo was not sad because he had just been told to get out or because he had just been called a great awful beastie by the Doctor. People were always saying things like that about him and it didn't bother him because he knew that no matter what anyone said, the Little Boy loved him and he loved the Little Boy. They were best friends and they played many games and had many adventures together. Sometimes Aldo was a horse and sometimes a camel, sometimes he was a fellow Cowboy or the fiery steed of a proud Knight. But the times he liked best were when he was just Aldo the sheepdog, whose best friend was the Little Boy. They cuddled and wrestled and the Little Boy would scratch his ears or rub his tummy and Aldo would give him big wet slurpy sheepdog kisses that made the Little Boy

giggle and the Little Boy's mother say, "Oh, Aldo, 41
that's disgusting."

"It's not disgusting, Mother," the Little Boy would answer. "It's a kiss."

Whereupon Aldo would usually kiss him again, wag his
tail happily, look at the Little Boy's mother and say Heh-
ah-heh-ah-heh-ah. The Little Boy loved it when he did
that and he would look at Aldo and open his own mouth
and stick out his own tongue and say Heh-ah-heh-ah-
heh-ah right back. Perhaps that was one of the reasons
that Aldo and the Little Boy were such good friends, for
the Little Boy knew that Aldo was part human just as
Aldo knew that the Little Boy, his best friend, was part
puppy.

So when the Doctor said, "Ooooof, great awful
beastic," it didn't matter to Aldo. That was not the reason
that his tail had stopped wagging, nor was it the reason
that he walked off in such a funk.

No, the reason was that when he had kissed the Little
Boy with his great wet slurpy kiss, just like the Little Boy's
mother, Aldo had noticed how hot his friend's forehead
was, how feverish his skin felt and how instead of gig-
gling, the Little Boy just lay there and barely smiled at all.

"His fever is very high," the Doctor said, shaking his
head and looking at the thermometer. "Dangerously high,
I'm afraid."

The Little Boy's mother looked down at her child and
brushed her fingers against his forehead as she fought
back tears.

"Now, now," said the Doctor, kindly putting his hand on her shoulder.

"Shouldn't . . . shouldn't we perhaps take him to hospital?" asked the Little Boy's mother.

"Yes," the Doctor said, "perhaps." He looked out the window briefly. In the distance he saw smoke still rising near the river from the bombing that had taken place the night before. "But with the way the hospitals have been targeted lately he's probably safer here."

"Yes," said the Little Boy's mother, "but couldn't they do more for him in hospital than we can do for him here?"

"I'm afraid not, ma'am," said the Doctor sadly. "The only thing to do is use cold compresses to try to bring the fever down and . . ." His voice trailed off.

"And what?" said the Little Boy's mother.

"And pray, ma'am," said the Doctor. Then he added quickly, "The boy's father has been sent for, I take it?"

The Little Boy's mother nodded and dabbed at her eyes with her handkerchief.

"Yes," she said, "they've been trying to locate him in order to arrange for an emergency leave."

The Little Boy stirred. He rolled his head back and forth on the pillow, opened his eyes, looked wildly about, then closed them again and said, "Davin."

"What's that?" asked the Doctor. "What's that he just said?"

The Little Boy's mother was weary with fatigue and worry.

"Davin," she said. "He's said it before. I don't know what it means. I think it's something to do with a game he played with his father."

"Where's Davin?" the Little Boy cried out in anguish.

His mother sat on the edge of his bed, took a cold cloth from the washbasin on his night table, wrung it out and put it on his forehead.

"Sweetheart," she said, "I don't know who Davin is." She reached for a little package she had put down on the night table when she'd entered the room. "Look," she said, "this came in the post today. It's from your father. He sent it almost a week ago. Let me open it for you."

The Little Boy turned to look at her and tried to focus his eyes as she opened the little package and pulled from it a tiny lead figure.

"It's Perseus," she said, "the Greek hero . . . see?"

She held the toy up so that the Little Boy could see the lead figure. He wore a short tunic and had a sword in his belt. The Little Boy reached out his hand and whispered, "Perseus."

"Is that the one who looks like me?" asked Yoni, suddenly perking up and sitting upright in his bed.

"Yes," said Grandma Goddess, "that's the one who looks exactly like you."

"Let Grandma Goddess read!" said Danielle.

"Shhhhh," said Adam, and then he added, "Go ahead, Grandma."

Grandma Goddess adjusted her reading glasses, looked back down at the book, found her spot and continued.

"At that same moment," she read, "Princess Helen was trying to hoist herself up out of the shoe box, which had been placed on the uppermost shelf of the back wall of the attic. Unfortunately for Princess Helen, the Nanny could not have chosen a worse place to put the shoe box. It probably made sense to her at the time, to put the shoe box full of toys next to another old discarded toy. Unfortunately she had placed it next to . . . the Pirate Ship— and not just any pirate ship. It was Blackbeard's ship. Blackbeard was the most terrifying toy of the lot. His men followed him out of fear and he had not a single friend, neither in the toy chest nor in the attic. Except for one . . . the Dark Knight. Now, as Princess Helen slid the lid off the top of the shoe box, she saw in front of her the fiercest-looking Pirate she had ever seen. He wore a patch over his eye and a hideous scar ran across his face.

"Aaarrr, my lass," Blackbeard said, and smiled, showing his brown and rotted teeth, "we've been expecting ye."

A long dark shadow fell over the Princess and the Pirate. Princess Helen looked up to see the Dark Knight towering above them, his eyes, it seemed, glowing red behind his helmet. "Seize them," his voice boomed.

From all directions, Pirates began streaming into the shoe box. Filthy Pirates who had not bathed in years and stank of sweat and dirt and the sea. Pirates who had never brushed their teeth and whose breath reeked every time they opened their mouths to yell, "Aaarrrr!" In the wink of an eye, the motley band of heroes found themselves bound hand and foot so that they could not move and with gags in their mouths so that they could not speak. And try as she might to escape, Princess Helen was brought by two Headless Horsemen to the Dark Knight and Blackbeard aboard the Pirate Ship. The Princess strained against the rope that bound her wrists together.

"You are only wasting your strength, Your Highness," sneered the Dark Knight. "Escape is impossible. Tomorrow you will either tell us where Davin lives or you will die."

"Aaaarrrr!" Blackbeard chimed in.

"I'm not afraid of you or your inarticulate friend," Princess Helen said.

But the truth was, she was very much afraid.

8

The Quest

Grandma Goddess closed the book.

"Grandma, what are you doing?" Yoni asked indignantly.

"I'm closing the book," said Grandma Goddess. "Then I'm going to make myself a cup of tea and then I'm going to bed."

"But what about Princess Helen?" Yoni asked.

"And what about the Little Boy?" asked Danielle.

"And what about Aldo?" said Adam, for Adam loved dogs more than almost anything else.

"They'll all stay just exactly where they are," said Grandma Goddess. "That's the wonderful thing about books. The stories are in them, ready whenever you are, waiting just the way you left them.

"Good night. I love you," Grandma Goddess said as she kissed three little foreheads.

"Criminitly," Yoni said.

"Isn't that a revolting development," said Danielle.

Adam didn't say anything. He was already on his way to Mars.

The next day could not go fast enough to suit the three children.

Finally . . . *finally* it was dinnertime. Yoni, Adam and Danielle raced through the meal. Grandma made her famous Grandma Goddess meatballs and her carrot ring. There was rice and fresh peas, which they had spent the afternoon shucking together.

After dinner, Yoni and Adam's father said, "Anyone want to watch some TV?"

"Nope."

"Nope."

"Nope," came the three answers.

Adam and Yoni's father turned to their mother.

"Anyone want to play a board game?" asked their mother.

"Nope."

"Early night."

"Goin' to bed," came the three replies.

"Well then," said the boys' father to Grandma Goddess, "would it be all right with you if we went out to the movies?"

"If it wouldn't be too much trouble to handle the kids by yourself," added the boys' mother.

"What do you think I am," asked Grandma Goddess, "feeble?"

So Yoni and Adam's mother and father went out to see some European movie that had no action at all and where the people just talked and ate snails or fish eggs, while Grandma Goddess and Yoni, Adam and Danielle cleared the dishes, rinsed them, put them in the dishwasher and put the leftovers in plastic containers and into the refrigerator. Then out came the cookies and hot chocolate and just as Grandma Goddess had told them, all the characters were there waiting, right where they had left them in the book.

Yoni, Adam and Danielle got their jammies on and cuddled into their blankets. They squished their pillows and slurped their hot chocolate. They smacked their lips out loud and said "Ahhhhh," then wiped off their chocolate mustaches.

Grandma Goddess put on her reading glasses and opened the book and began to read.

That night the Little Boy slept fitfully. All day long after the Doctor had left, his mother swabbed him with cold cloths soaked in ice water and alcohol. He shivered and tossed and turned. He was what they called delirious.

"What's that mean?" Adam asked.

"Well," said Grandma Goddess, "it means he wasn't thinking too straight."

"It means he was goofy," Yoni said.

"Yes," said Grandma Goddess, "that's about it. He was kind of goofy because he was very sick. He didn't know if the things he was seeing were real or make-believe. He was delirious."

She traced down the page with her finger looking for her place and when she found it she went on.

Finally that night he slipped into a fitful sleep. His eyes would close and he would doze off, then be awake, then doze again until he could no longer tell the difference and his dreams seemed as real to him as anything that was actually happening when he was awake. And the things that were happening when he was awake seemed as strange and unreal to him as his dreams.

His poor mother tried to stay awake and keep watch over him, but she was exhausted. The Nanny was no help. She had already gone to sleep and you could even hear her snoring through the floorboards. When the Little Boy's mother saw the Little Boy doze off, she allowed herself to sit back in her chair. "I'll just take a little nap," she thought, and before she could finish the thought in her mind, she was asleep.

At that very moment, the Little Bugle Boy and the Blustery Sergeant Major crawled up out of the deep fold in the blue blanket and made their way up toward the pillow where the little toy figure of Perseus lay next to the Little Boy's head. Perseus looked at them with a leaden look, since lead was what he was made of.

"Dull fellow," said the Blustery Sergeant Major, "very dull fellow indeed."

Just then the Little Boy opened his eyes and said, "Princess Helen . . . have . . . to . . . help Princess . . . Helen . . ."

"Yes, well," said the Blustery Sergeant Major. "It's all

very well and good for him to say you have to help Princess Helen . . . All he has to do is lie here. We're the ones who would have to face the danger if we were foolish enough to try!"

"We have to do something," said the brave Little Bugle Boy.

"Nothing of the kind," said the Sergeant Major. "We're completely outnumbered. We haven't reconnoitered the area. We haven't a plan. Completely unsound tactics, my lad. Completely unsound!" he said, and harrummphed and ahemmed and harrummphed once again for good measure.

"Well, maybe *he* can help," said the Bugle Boy, and he looked over at Perseus, who lay stiff as a board, staring motionlessly into the sky.

"Him?" said the Sergeant Major. "Him? Old Lead-in-the Pants? I hardly think so. He's stiff as a dead mullet. Stiff as old Skully Joe. I'm afraid he isn't real."

"Why not?" asked the Bugle Boy.

"Because Perseus has never been played with. Toys are only real if a child has played with them or pretended with them. If a child does not believe in a toy, it isn't alive. It is the Little Boy who makes us real."

But before the Sergeant Major could finish his sentence, a truly remarkable thing occurred. The Little Boy turned his head on his pillow and whispered, "Perseus . . . help me . . . ," and just as he said the word "Perseus," the little lead figure's coloring improved and his skin began to soften from a dull shipyard gray to something quite, well, . . . real-looking. He blinked and blinked again, and his big brown eyes darted to the left and to the right. With his right pinky he tapped his leg once . . . twice . . . three times. He wiggled his fingers and wriggled his toes. He crinkled his nose. His muscles flexed under his tunic and he raised one arm and then the other. Then he put them both down and his lips turned up into a smile. The great hero bent his strong knee and put one foot forward and then . . . he fell flat on his back. But he slowly got to his feet and tried to walk once again. And although he stumbled, he caught his balance and managed to take another step and then another until it appeared he had the hang of it. The Sergeant Major and the Bugle Boy had been watching in awe and when Perseus took his third step they both began to applaud. Perseus smiled and turned to them and said, "Ahweewee." He had not yet gotten the knack of speaking and a discouraged look came across his face as he realized he had not said what he wanted to say. He tried again, "Ahweewee."

"Slow down, my boy," the Sergeant Major said.

Perseus concentrated very hard and said, "Ah . . . wee . . . wee."

"My dear boy," sighed the Sergeant Major, becoming a bit exasperated himself, "you must enunciate."

"I think he's doing very well for just having been born," said the Bugle Boy. "He's talking baby talk."

But Perseus did not want to talk baby talk. He wanted to talk like a real hero. So he tried one last time and said, "I feel real!"

"Well, hurrah for you," said the Sergeant Major.

The Bugle Boy grabbed Perseus's arm and began pulling on it, saying, "Come on. What are we waiting for? We have to go to the attic and find the great Davin and save the Little Boy. Let's go!"

"Oh bosh, tosh, poof and piffle," said the Blustery Sergeant Major. "It's going to take a good deal more than 'Ahweewee' to face the Dark Knight! You're both defective merchandise, if you ask me. To the attic indeed! We don't even know where the attic is. This is a most unsound expedition."

"It isn't an expedition," said the Bugle Boy. "It's a quest. It's an adventure."

"An adventure!" repeated Perseus, for Perseus wanted to have many adventures. But then he began to consider the circumstances and said, "I want to go to attics and face Dark Knights and save the Little Boy and have adventures, but I just became real. I haven't even tried running yet."

"But we don't have any time to waste," the Bugle Boy said urgently. "We have to find El Lobo and save the Princess and get Davin—"

"Did you say Princess?" asked Perseus, interrupting the Little Bugle Boy.

"Yes. Princess Helen," said the Bugle Boy impatiently. "She's the only one who knows where to find Davin."

"Is she . . . pretty?" asked Perseus.

"She's only the most beautiful girl in the shoe box," said the Bugle Boy, "but I don't see what that has to do with anything."

Perseus's interest was piqued. "Does she have a good personality and a kind heart?"

The Sergeant Major shook his head and sighed. "She has a charming personality. A wonderful personality, but—"

Perseus had heard all he needed to hear. "To the attic!" he shouted.

"To the attic!" cried the Bugle Boy.

"Now, now, wait a minute," puffed the Sergeant Major. "It's all well and good to talk of adventures and Princesses, but we are only three and the Dark Knight has a whole army. I for one am not about to embark on this journey to disaster."

"Look," said the Little Bugle Boy, "if you don't want to come, then stay here. But I'm going. We have to do something!"

"Go ahead," said the Blustery Sergeant Major. "Go ahead and get yourselves lost and broken beyond repair. See if I care!"

"Fine," said the Bugle Boy.

"Fine indeed," said the Sergeant Major.

"You're very brave," said Perseus to the Sergeant Major.

"Of course I am," said the Sergeant Major, who had never been called brave before. "I am?"

"Oh yes, indeed," Perseus said. "After all, you'll be the only toy left in the nursery now."

"I will?" said the Sergeant Major. He looked around. It was true. The Nanny had packed off all the other figures into the shoe box. Only the Sergeant Major and the Bugle Boy had been able to avoid being shipped to the attic.

"Yes," said the Bugle Boy, "all alone in the dark . . . with that horrible gargoyle staring down at you."

"Yes . . . ," said the Sergeant Major, who was beginning to feel lonely and frightened already.

"Well," said the Bugle Boy, "bye-bye."

"Eh . . . Ahem . . . ," the Blustery Sergeant Major blustered, "on second thought, you two are nothing but puppies. You need someone with sufficient maturity and judgment, not to mention years of military discipline and experience, to keep you out of trouble."

And so the Bugle Boy, the Blustery Sergeant Major and Perseus, the young Greek hero, set off for that strange and faraway place called . . . the attic!

9

The Hallway

"What's that?" asked the Blustery Sergeant Major. "What's what?" asked Perseus.

They had only gone a few paces out of the Little Boy's room into the hallway when the Sergeant Major stopped dead in his tracks, looked all around into the darkness and said, "What's that?"

"I don't hear anything," the Bugle Boy said. He adjusted the bugle on its golden cord so that it hung just right off his shoulder. This was the first time he had ever been on a real adventure. All the rest had been on the Little Boy's bed. But this was different and he wanted to make sure he looked very regimental. He hooked his thumbs inside his belt the way he had seen the Cowboys do and looked all around.

"That!" said the Blustery Sergeant Major. "Listen!"

The three of them stood there and listened as hard as

they could, and sure enough there were all kinds of sounds. In the distance they could hear the air raid warden's whistle as he scolded people to put up their blackout curtains or douse their lights. There was the occasional sound of a passing motorcar and there were creaks and groans, the creaks and groans of an old house, the drip drip drip of a leaky faucet somewhere and . . .

"There it is again," said the Sergeant Major.

This time they all heard it. It was a low sound that seemed to go rrrrrrrrrr in the darkness. It would stop for a second as if taking a breath and then go rrrrrrrrrrr again.

"Oh well," said the Little Bugle Boy, "that's probably just a . . ."

"Probably just a what?" the Sergeant Major demanded.

"Probably just something that wants nothing to do with us," said Perseus, trying to be brave, though it was obvious he was none too sure of himself.

"Oh, just what was called for," said the Sergeant Major, "the expert opinion of someone whose entire life experience is what . . . about fifteen minutes if I'm not mistaken?"

"Let's just go," said the Bugle Boy.

"Go!" exclaimed the Blustery Sergeant Major. He shook his jowls and puffed up red-cheeked like a blowfish. He poofed out a puff of air and said, "Phuuuuuuuuuhhh-hhh, and where, might I be so bold as to ask, do you think it is that we should be going?"

"To the attic," Perseus said heroically.

"To the attic! Brilliant. And where, you twit, *is* the attic?" he demanded. "Hmmmmm?"

"Well," said the Little Bugle Boy, "when the Nanny was taking us there she said she was going . . ." He paused and scratched his head and then announced proudly, "Up!"

"Up," said the Sergeant Major.

"Up," said the Bugle Boy.

There was a long silence and then the Sergeant Major said, "Right . . . well . . . it's a start at least."

Perseus, the Bugle Boy and the Sergeant Major walked all the way to the end of the hall until they came to the first set of stairs, which led to the second landing.

Each step was easily three times as tall as the Bugle Boy. Not even Perseus was tall enough to reach up to the top of even the first step. He suggested that perhaps the Sergeant Major could give him a boost.

"Right," said the Sergeant Major. "Right as rain."

He stood with his back braced against the step and sort of squatted back against it to get an even firmer footing. He laced his fingers together until his hands formed a kind of stirrup and he held them out toward Perseus.

"Right," he said. "Up we go, my lad."

"I'll stand guard," said the Little Bugle Boy proudly, and he clutched his bugle as if it were a weapon.

"Well," the Sergeant Major said, "I feel ever so much safer now."

Perseus stepped up and put his right foot into the Sergeant Major's stirrup made of laced fingers. He put his hands onto the Sergeant Major's shoulders.

The Sergeant Major said, "One . . . two . . . threeeee!"

He heaved and the young Greek hero Perseus reached up as high as he could, but his fingers still didn't reach the top of the step.

"Let's try it again," he said.

The Sergeant Major's cheeks puffed in and out like a bellows and his face was red as a beet, red as a cherry or a red-hot fireplace poker.

"Right," he said through clenched teeth, "right. We'll just try again. But this time, give it a bit more oomph! What do you say, lad? Really step into it!"

"Right," said Perseus.

"Right," said the Sergeant Major. "And one . . . two . . . threeee!" he said, and heaved with all his might.

When the Sergeant Major heaved, Perseus not only reached up as far as he could, he did exactly what the Sergeant Major said he should. He tried to step into it. He lifted up his right foot and planted it firmly on the Sergeant Major's head.

"Mind the head, you twit, mind the head!" the Sergeant Major said. Perseus reached up on his tiptoes on top of the Sergeant Major's pillbox hat and the pillbox hat slipped forward and down into the Sergeant Major's eyes.

"Oooooof," said the Sergeant Major.

Perseus lifted up his other foot until both feet were standing precariously on the Sergeant Major's head.

"Bhhhhhouuu!" said the Sergeant Major.

"Almost there," said Perseus.

The Sergeant Major, however, had begun to slide down under Perseus's weight so the Little Bugle Boy quickly leaned his shoulder into the Sergeant Major's stomach to help prop him up.

"Oooooof," said the Sergeant Major as all the wind was knocked out of him.

"Got it!" shouted Perseus.

Perseus's fingers tightened around the top of the step and he pulled himself up off the Sergeant Major's head and onto the first step.

Next the Sergeant Major boosted up the Little Bugle Boy.

"One . . . two . . . three," he said, and boosted the Little Bugle Boy up so easily that he flew up over the top of the step and landed squarely on top of Perseus and knocked him flat as a squished bug.

The next part was a little more difficult. Perseus and the Bugle Boy at first tried pulling the Sergeant Major up.

The Sergeant Major stood on his tiptoes.

Perseus and the Little Bugle Boy reached down.

The Sergeant Major reached up.

They each took one of his hands and then huffed and puffed, pulled and strained, yanked, jerked, heaved and ho'ed with all their might.

Instead of their pulling the Sergeant Major up, the Sergeant Major almost succeeded in toppling the two of them head over heels off the step and back down to where they had started from.

"Your rope," the Bugle Boy said to Perseus.

"My what?" said Perseus.

"Your rope," said the Bugle Boy. "Isn't that what that is in your belt?"

Perseus looked down and indeed there was a silver cord, coiled up and looped through his belt next to the scabbard that held his sword. He tied one end around the banister. The Sergeant Major climbed up with the aid of the rope until Perseus and the Bugle Boy could reach down and grab an arm. He kicked off with his feet against the step and pulled with all his might as Perseus and the Bugle Boy pulled with all *their* might and up he went finally over the top of the first step.

That was the way they made it up to the landing. The Sergeant Major boosted first Perseus and then the Bugle Boy. Then they tied off the rope and lowered it down and helped the Sergeant Major up each step. Finally the three of them stood together on the landing, looking down at how far they had come, when suddenly they heard it again.

"Rrrrrrrrrrrr."

"What is that?" said the Sergeant Major.

"I don't know," Perseus said.

"I do!" said the Bugle Boy. "Look out!"

They looked up and there across the landing was the

Nanny's fat tabby cat. The rrrrrrrrrrr . . . rrrrrrrrrrr
sound grew louder and louder. It was not a contented
purrrrrrrrrrring sound . . . it was a hungry one! It was
in fact the sound of the cat-word for "lunch"!

The fat cat licked her chops, ran her tongue across her
fangs and dug her claws into the carpet, as if testing them,
sharpening them for the kill. To the Nanny's cat, the
three figures didn't look like toys at all, they looked just
like three plump juicy little mice ready to be eaten!

10

The Nanny's Cat

"Okay," said Grandma Goddess, closing the book. "That will do it for tonight."

"But Grandma Goddess—" said Danielle.

"Good night, my sweet children," Grandma Goddess said. She got up and crossed over to the lamp and started to turn it out.

"Grandma Goddess, this isn't fair," said Yoni, who had a very highly developed sense of justice when it came to bedtime stories.

"What's not fair?"

"They're about to be eaten!" Yoni declared. "They're going to be turned into Cat Chow! You can't just get up in the middle of something like that."

Grandma Goddess had turned to Yoni and did not see Adam sneaking out of his bed, but that is just what he did. He crossed over behind Grandma Goddess to the door that led out into the hall.

"I'll read you the rest tomorrow," Grandma Goddess said, but when she turned, there was Adam in front of her with his back against the closed door and his arms spread out across the door and the wall.

"You can't leave, Grandma Goddess, until we find out about the cat." And then he added the one word that made all the difference in the world. *"Please,"* he said.

"Ah," said Grandma Goddess, *"please . . .* well, I suppose that's something else again. That's something that no one thought to say until now."

"Please, oh please, Grandma Goddess," Danielle said.

"Pleeeeeeeeeeeeeeeeeeeeeeeeeeeease!" said Yoni.

"Five minutes more," said Grandma Goddess. "Five minutes and not a minute more."

"Have a seat," Yoni said, moving the chair back out for his grandmother.

Grandma Goddess sat down, smiling. Then she opened up the book and began once again to read.

The fat cat licked her chops, ran her tongue across her fangs and dug her claws into the carpet, as if testing them, sharpening them for the kill. To the Nanny's cat, the three figures didn't look like toys at all, they looked just like three plump juicy little mice ready to be eaten!

"Run for your lives!" shouted the Sergeant Major, looking around wildly for someplace to run.

There in the corner, hidden in the shadows, they could

see what looked like a tiny tunnel entrance, just beneath the light socket.

"It's a mouse hole!" Perseus shouted.

"Mouse hole, shmouse hole!" said the Sergeant Major. "I don't care what it is, as long as that monster can't get us there. To the rear . . . charge!"

So saying, the Sergeant Major began running as fast as his plump stubby little legs could carry him.

At the opposite end of the hallway, the Nanny's fat tabby cat seemed positively to smile. She swung her tail back and forth, arched her back, and sank down low on her haunches. Then in one swift incredibly powerful move, she sprang from where she sat, flying headlong up and out through the air, and came down on her four paws in full gallop.

If there is anything that is true in life at all, it is that no human being can ever fully understand what a cat is thinking. Cats are not people, that's why they call them cats. But while it is not possible to *know* what a cat is thinking, it may indeed be possible to *suppose* one's way into the feline mind. So put yourself in the fat tabby's position. You look down the hall and you see something short and stubby with a juicy potbelly and a handlebar mustache that looks remarkably whiskerlike. What do you think it is?

"A mouse!" said Adam definitely.

"Adam," Yoni said, "she wasn't asking you, she was reading the story."

"Oh," said Adam.

"That's all right," said Grandma Goddess. "When you read a story to someone, it becomes their story, too. So if someone asks a question and you want to answer it, why not?" Then she looked back down at the page and found her place once again.

". . . something short and stubby with a juicy pot-belly and a handlebar mustache that looks remarkably whiskerlike. What do you think it is?"

"A mouse!" shouted Yoni, Danielle and Adam all together.

"A mouse," said Grandma Goddess, "especially if the short and stubby legs and the juicy plump potbelly and the very mouselike whiskers are now running toward what you know perfectly well is a mouse's hole."

And even though it is impossible to know for certain what the tabby cat was thinking, it would be a good guess to say that as the Nanny's tabby galloped madly down the hall after the Blustery Sergeant Major, she was thinking *Snacktime snacktime snacktime snacktime.*

By comparison, it is not at all difficult to know what the Blustery Sergeant Major was thinking at that same time.

"*Hhhhheeeeeeeeeeeelllllllllpppp!*" yelled the Blustery Sergeant Major.

He was a little more than two feet away from the mouse's hole now and perhaps that fact alone should have been encouraging. The problem, however, was that the Nanny's hungry tabby cat was *less* than two feet away from *him!*

Perseus watched as the cat got closer. One more bounding leap and she would be able to pounce upon the Sergeant Major. Here was Perseus's first chance for a battle, his first heroic adventure. He drew his sword and stood right in the cat's path and let out a loud war whoop, as he supposed a hero should before going into battle. His sword was poised and he was ready to fight.

The cat, however, simply bounded over him, choosing not to stop to deal with what must have looked to her like very skimpy pickings indeed, compared to the juicy Sergeant Major. Perseus was left standing with sword in hand, confused about what had gone wrong.

The Blustery Sergeant Major ran as fast as he could, but just then the Nanny's cat pounced. She went up through the air and came down with her paw flat against the Sergeant Major's back, sending him sprawling to the floor.

The cat now rested on her haunches, her paw pinning the Sergeant Major to the carpet.

"Purrrrrrrrrrrr . . . ," said the cat. She ran her tongue across her teeth, opened her mouth wide and leaned her head forward, about to take the first juicy bite out of the Sergeant Major.

The Little Bugle Boy watched in horror. He had to do something or his friend would be eaten. But what could he do? He had no sword or rifle. All he had was a bugle.

"Dot da dot da dot da dot da dot da dot da dot da dot daaaaaaaa . . ." He blew the cavalry charge with all his might, and held out one long last note as loud as he possibly could. It was an impossibly high-pitched call to battle, the kind that could rouse any group of fighting men from their slumber and inspire them to charge the enemy. The only problem was . . . he didn't have an army.

The cat turned and looked at him and for the tiniest instant was actually afraid, never having heard a cavalry charge played in her ear before.

The Little Bugle Boy saw the look of fear and thought, "It's working!" And so he played the charge again. "Dot da dot da dot da dot da dot da dot da dot da dot daaaaaaaaaaaaaaaaaaaaaaaaaaaaaaaaaaaaaaaaaaaaa . . . ," holding the last note out even longer and higher-pitched than before.

Unfortunately, though, the second charge didn't frighten the Nanny's fat tabby cat. Instead she caught the rhythm of the tune and actually enjoyed it. She began nodding her head in time to the music and humming along with it! "Hmm hmm hmmm hmmm hmmm hmm hmmm hmmm hmmmm hmmm hmmm hmmm hmmm hmmm hmmmmmmmmmmmmm . . .

"Ahhhh," thought the cat, "music for dining."

And she scooped the Sergeant Major toward her open jaws.

The cat, however, was not the only one to hear the Little Bugle Boy's last high-pitched wailing cry for help.

Galooomph galooomph galooomph galooomph came Aldo's paws, galloping up the stairs, across the landing.

"Grrrrrrrr . . . ," he growled menacingly at the sight of the cat.

The tabby looked up with a terrified expression and squeaked pleadingly, "Meow?"

"Woof woof woof, you miserable stinking tabby cat!" Aldo barked as he raced headlong toward her.

The cat screeched and jumped straight into the air, hit the handrail and jumped two full flights down the stairs with the huge shaggy dog in hot pursuit. With the cat for the moment gone, the Little Bugle Boy and Perseus picked the Sergeant Major up underneath his arms and ran with him as fast as they could to the safety of the mouse's hole.

11

The Attic

"Good night," said Grandma Goddess.

She kissed Yoni on the forehead, whispered, "Good night," and said, "You're growing to be a very big boy, you know?"

"Uh-huh," said Yoni.

Grandma Goddess always said something to each of the children, each time in a whisper for only that child to hear. It might be about how big they were growing or what nice penmanship they had. It might be about their manners or something kind they had done that day for someone. It might be about sports or Danielle's dancing. Whatever it was, it was always something that was just about them and that let them know Grandma Goddess thought whatever was important to them was important to her.

"Good night," she said to Danielle, and whispered

something secret in her ear and then kissed her forehead. Whatever she whispered made Danielle giggle and say, "Oh goody."

"Good night," Grandma Goddess said to Adam, and whispered something secret in his ear and kissed his forehead as well.

The next day, Adam and Danielle and Yoni complained that they were bored and had nothing to do. They wanted to go to the beach but there was no one to take them. There were no good movies out and they were just plain bored with no one to entertain them. Grandma Goddess wasn't there because she had gone to visit some friends for the day. Finally Adam got an idea. He started to draw pictures. Then Danielle saw what he was drawing and she began to draw, too.

They drew pictures of the adventures of the Bugle Boy and the Blustery Sergeant Major and Perseus, while Yoni played action figure games of the same adventures. Then Yoni thought it would be fun to make a movie about those same adventures. He put the action figures on the stairs and used string for Perseus's rope. The difficulty was that the children had no cat.

They did have a little white fluffy dog named Scraps on whom Danielle tied cat ears. They tried every way possible to get Scraps to attack the action figures for the video camera, but the only things he would attack were the cat ears Danielle had tied around his head. He rolled on the floor and scratched at them with his paws and once they were off his head he barked at them ferociously, then picked them up in his mouth and ran away.

"Cut!" said Yoni in disgust. He ran to the cupboard in the kitchen and grabbed a dog biscuit. He ran back to where the action figures were and placed them on top of the biscuit so that when Scraps bent down to eat the biscuit, it looked as if he were trying to eat Perseus, the Bugle Boy and the Sergeant Major. Adam and Danielle did all the voices and the sound effects and by the time Yoni and Adam's mother got home they were almost finished with the scene.

"How was your day?" Yoni and Adam's mother asked. She expected to hear three whiny voices saying how boring the day had been.

Instead she heard, "It was great!"

"It was the best!"

"We made a movie!"

"Great!" said Yoni and Adam's mother. "Can I see it? We can even make some popcorn and—"

"Well," said Yoni, "I haven't edited it yet."

"That's okay," his mother said. "Let me just see what you've shot."

Yoni stood up straight with a very serious look on his face. Movies were not something he took lightly. "I'm sorry," he said, "but I never show my dailies."

That night after dinner, the children helped clean up and then gathered in Yoni's room to listen to Grandma Goddess read.

It was very very dark inside the mouse's hole. The Little Bugle Boy and the Blustery Sergeant Major and Perseus stood there trying to catch their breaths. Gradually their eyes began to adjust to the dark.

"Look," said the Little Bugle Boy, pointing up.

The Blustery Sergeant Major and Perseus looked up to where the Bugle Boy was pointing. Above them, at what seemed a very great distance, was a tiny pinpoint of light.

"I bet that's where the attic is!" the Bugle Boy said. "I bet that's where the light is coming from!"

"You don't *know* that to be the case," said the Blustery Sergeant Major. "In fact, you don't *know* anything to be the case!"

"Yes, well, I *do* know one thing," the Little Bugle Boy said.

"Really, what's that?" said the Blustery Sergeant Major disdainfully.

"I know that the Nanny's cat is out there!" the Bugle Boy said, pointing through the mouse hole out into the hallway.

"Yes," said the Blustery Sergeant Major, "well, perhaps it would be best to investigate the source of that light after all. Fair enough, men, let's go."

On the inside of the wall there were a series of wooden slats almost like a ladder that led straight up. In addition, there were electrical wires that circled and snaked their way up the insides of the walls, which Perseus climbed like a monkey. The Little Bugle Boy and

the Sergeant Major watched in awe as Perseus found a
way to climb over every obstacle, going hand over hand
up the electrical wiring. He would point out the places
for them to plant their feet, the best way to climb and
where they could rest and catch their breaths. Slowly
but surely, the three of them made their way closer and
closer to the light.

The nearer they got to it, the larger it appeared, until
finally they could see that it was a hole very similar to the
mouse hole in the hallway, except this one led out into
that great dark mysterious place they had only heard
of . . . the attic.

Perseus was the first to pull himself through the hole;
then came the Little Bugle Boy, and together they helped
pull the Sergeant Major through the opening and out
onto the attic floor. The light they had seen was the glow
from a night-light plugged into one of the sockets near
the mouse hole. When they took a few steps out into the
attic, however, the light was behind them and of no use at
all.

How dark the attic was! It seemed to go on and on, as
endless as pictures of outer space in the Little Boy's adventure books. Yet as they moved forward, they had the
uncanny feeling that they were not alone and that they
were being watched. To one side was an old and broken
lamp base without a shade.

On the base there was the figure of a woman carrying a
huge water jug on her head. But the strangest thing hap-

pened. If they took three steps to the left, the eyes of the woman with the jug seemed to follow them to the left. If they took the same number of paces to the right, the eyes of the woman with the jug followed them to the right. She watched them like a school librarian watching a noisy child. And it wasn't just the woman with the jug; there was the face on a china plate and the mug with the broken handle and the red-cheeked *Bürgermeister*'s face. His eyes followed them, too. As did the eyes of the silver lizard that adorned the discarded serving bowl. The truth was that everything in the attic was alive and watching them. The Little Bugle Boy, the Sergeant Major and Perseus were the intruders and the attic itself seemed immediately to know that they were there. Spiders stopped in their webs, mice stopped nibbling and sniffed the air, faces in long-forgotten photographs behind cracked glass in dusty frames turned to look at them.

Then, out of the darkness, they noticed something else watching them as well. First two, then four, then six glowing red dots appeared in the dark. They were in pairs. One pair here, then suddenly one pair there and then a third pair, all seeming to circle and take up position as if to surround them.

"That's no *Bürgermeister* mug," said the Little Bugle Boy.

"That's no face on a china plate, either," said the Sergeant Major with a shudder.

"Whatever they are," said Perseus, "they're alive and they're trouble." He pulled his sword out of its sheath.

The Little Bugle Boy clutched at his bugle and the Sergeant Major looked around furtively for someplace to hide.

Then the creatures sprang at them from out of the darkness, three giant wicked-looking rats, their claws slashing out, their huge sharp fanglike teeth bared, their giant tails like snakes thrashing as white foam dripped from their jaws. Each one of them was as big as the Nanny's tabby cat and many times more ferocious-looking. The lead rat rose on its hind legs and then swiped out with its claws extended like a set of slashing knives, cutting through the air, whizzing next to Perseus's face. Perseus swung with his sword, held it in both hands and swung with all his might into the soft fleshy part of the rat's paw, behind its claws. The rat screeched in pain and slashed again, its claws ripping into Perseus's hands and sending his sword flying. The Bugle Boy and the Sergeant Major stood behind Perseus but now he had nothing with which to defend them as the other two rats closed in from the left and from the right. Now there was no way out and nothing they could do against these giant venomous monster rats, who smiled to one another as they drew closer . . . and closer.

Just then Perseus heard a sound that sounded something like thungggg. It was the sound of something very tight that had just been sprung.

Then the Bugle Boy heard a similar sound but this one coming from a different place. Thunggg! Then the sound of something flying, whizzing past him, whooshing through the air.

Then there was a thwappp and thwapp again as two arrows flew out of the darkness, thwapping straight into the shoulder of the giant rat.

12

New Friends

The rat spun back, rearing on its hind legs and tail, its claws lashing out and head thrashing through the air. It let out a high-pitched banshee cry, looking like a dragon about to breathe fire. Then it came down straight for Perseus, clutching at the arrows with one set of giant claws and ripping them free. The rat's dripping jaws were less than an inch away from Perseus when there was heard once again that same sound.

Thunnggg! Swoosh! And then thwapp went the arrow, this time straight into the giant rat's ugly snout. Now the rat reared back in pain with the arrow protruding from the soft part of its nose. It turned and scampered back into the shadows, screeching in pain as it ran.

Perseus looked over his left shoulder. Stepping out toward them was a tall man dressed all in forest green with a forester's cap cocked at a jaunty angle. In his hands he held an English longbow. He reached behind his shoulder and unsheathed another arrow, nocked it, drew back the bowstring and . . . thungggg!

Swoosh! The arrow flew past Perseus.

Thwapp! It struck the second rat in its snout as well.

The rat jumped back, both paws pulling at the arrow, thrashing its head against the floor and trying to shake the arrow free.

The third rat meanwhile sank down low and scurried back into the darkness.

The Little Bugle Boy turned to look at whoever had just saved them.

There was another bowman on one knee holding a birch bow in his hand, and when he stood he looked to be at least a head taller than the one in the green cap. This second bowman wore leather moccasins and a breechcloth and across his chest a breastplate made of bones. He wore a leather headband and hanging from his mighty bow were eagle feathers and colored beads. He was bronze-skinned and war paint decorated his face.

"W-Who . . . ," stammered Perseus to the first bowman. "Who are you?"

"Who are *we*?" said the first bowman. "I should think the better question is who are the three of you and, more to the point, what are you doing here?"

"My name is Perseus," said the young Greek, "and my friends and I are on a very important mission." He picked up his sword and tore a piece of cloth off his tunic to bandage his arm.

"Important mission, eh?" said the bowman with the forester's cap on his head. "It's been quite some time since there's been anyone on an important mission up here. My name is Robin."

The Little Bugle Boy stared at him in awe. "Robin," he said. "Robin Hood?"

"The same," said Robin, doffing his cap.

"Oh posh tosh," sniffed the Sergeant Major. "And I suppose you're going to tell us this savage is Friar Tuck!"

The Little Bugle Boy poked the Sergeant Major in the ribs.

"I wouldn't call him a savage," the Bugle Boy said. "He might scalp us," he whispered, eyeing the tomahawk in the tall Indian's belt.

Robin spoke. "My friend's name is Chingachgook and he is the last of a very noble people known as the Mohicans."

"Ah," said the Sergeant Major, stepping up quickly. He turned to Chingachgook and spoke slowly, hoping that the red Indian would somehow understand his words. "Ahem," he said, clearing his throat importantly. "Us . . . plenty sorry. You . . . save-um our lives . . . We . . . plenty grateful."

Chingachgook gazed intently at the Sergeant Major. The Sergeant Major wasn't sure if the Indian had understood a word he'd said.

"You . . . understand-um? You . . . speakee English?" the Sergeant Major asked.

Chingachgook looked from the Sergeant Major to

Robin Hood. "I say," he said in a very British accent, "the portly chap's grammar is perfectly appalling." Then he turned to the Sergeant Major and spoke slowly and distinctly. "Yes," he said, "I speakee . . . English. You speakee English, too?"

The Sergeant Major huffed and puffed and sputtered and muttered, trying to contain his anger and embarrassment. "Speakee English," he said to himself. "Well, of course I speakee English!"

"Ah, well, there's a relief," said Chingachgook. He stuck out his hand to the Sergeant Major. "Delighted to make your acquaintance. Well," he said, looking from one of them to the other, "I don't know about you chaps but I could do with a spot of tea."

"Right," said Robin.

Chingachgook reached into his leather pouch and pulled out a teapot as Robin crouched low and struck up a small fire. As the two men went about boiling the water they explained to Perseus, the Bugle Boy and the Sergeant Major that they were two forgotten heroes.

"Playthings, actually," said Chingachgook somewhat wistfully. Robin Hood and Chingachgook told their new friends they had once belonged to the Little Boy's father and had been put up in the attic long long ago with the rest of his childhood toys. Robin had gotten separated from his band of Merry Men and Chingachgook from his good friend Hawkeye. Together the two of them now roamed about the attic, barely scratching out a living. They had been lonely years but at least Chingachgook had put them to good use reading all the homilies and sayings on the discarded sets of dishes that cluttered up the attic and listening every night on the old crystal set to the BBC, so that he had in fact developed a perfectly lovely accent and command of the English language.

His taste in music ran to Mozart, which was the cause of some disagreement with Robin Hood, who preferred American jazz, which Chingachgook regarded as almost barbaric.

After Chingachgook had poured the tea he turned to the Bugle Boy, Perseus and the Sergeant Major and said, "One lump or two?"

"One and a half, please," said the Bugle Boy.

"Ah," said Chingachgook, "waste not, want not." So saying, in the blink of an eye he whipped out his tomahawk and slashed through the lump of sugar, neatly cutting it in half.

Robin, Chingachgook, the Bugle Boy, the Sergeant Major and Perseus enjoyed their tea. Chingachgook inquired as to the nature of their mission. He and Robin sat and listened as the three told them about the Little Boy's sickness and his whispered plea to rescue the Princess Helen and somehow find Davin.

"And," said the Bugle Boy, "Princess Helen told us the one who could help us was El Lobo."

"El Lobo?" said Chingachgook, looking at Robin and stifling a laugh. "I shouldn't think he'd be of much use."

"Hardly," agreed Robin Hood.

Robin and Chingachgook explained to Perseus, the Bugle Boy and the Sergeant Major that they already knew about the Dark Knight and Princess Helen. They had watched as the Nanny waddled down the length of the attic muttering to herself that she was going to stick the shoe box up on the Shelves.

"The Shelves?" asked Perseus. "Where are they?"

"Bit of bad luck there, I'm afraid," said Chingachgook.

He explained that once there had been as many good toys in the attic as villains. The villains for the most part were the Pirates led by Blackbeard himself.

"Perfectly awful chap," Robin put in.

"Yes, quite," said Chingachgook. "And the problem of course is that his Pirate Ship is on the Shelves as well, you see?"

"So if the Dark Knight has now combined forces with Blackbeard and his Pirates," said Robin Hood, "any rescue attempt could be quite sticky."

As for Davin, both Robin and Chingachgook had certainly heard of him.

"But no one in the attic knows where he lives," said Robin. "No one except perhaps El Lobo, the doddering old Spaniard. He might know. He might know the way to the Shelves, for that matter."

"*Doddering* old Spaniard?" asked Perseus. "El Lobo the doddering old Spaniard?"

"Yes, well . . . and there's the problem, isn't it?" said Chingachgook. "I'm afraid El Lobo is long since past his prime."

13

El Lobo

Robin explained to Perseus, the Bugle Boy and the Sergeant Major that evil times had descended upon the attic. In the old days, long long ago in fact, things had been lovely. But then for some reason that none of the toys could ever understand things had become . . . well . . . he didn't quite know how to explain it. It was as if all of them had fallen into a deep deep sleep, almost as if they'd been put under some kind of spell, like in a fairy tale . . . like, oh, what was that story the Nanny was always prattling on about . . . "Sleeping Beauty." That was it! It was as if they were put under the same kind of spell as in the fairy tale. A great deal of time must have gone by and then they'd reawakened. Things had gone on rather swimmingly for a while but now that the Dark Knight and his men were in cahoots with Blackbeard and the Pirates, the situation had deteriorated, gone downhill quite drastically, actually. You could hear them at night from far away, drinking and shouting, carousing and in general behaving in the most uncivilized manner. The toys who were not themselves villains never even ventured out of the Fort anymore.

"What fort?" asked Perseus.

"I say," said Chingachgook, "you really are new in the woods . . . or the attic, as the case may be."

"The Fort," Robin explained, "is just exactly what it sounds like and unless I miss my guess that is exactly where one would find El Lobo. Wouldn't you say so?" he asked Chingachgook.

"Ra-ther," returned the last of the Mohicans.

"Could you take us there?" asked the Bugle Boy.

"Where?" said Robin pleasantly.

"Why, to the Fort, of course," the Bugle Boy answered.

"What? Us?" said Chingachgook.

"Take you?" said Robin.

"To the Fort?" said Chingachgook, completing his friend's thought.

"Yes," said Perseus.

"Whatever for?" Robin asked, sipping at his tea.

"It's a perfectly dreadful place," Chingachgook added, picking up the teapot and pouring just enough into his cup to require another lump of sugar, so that he looked to the Sergeant Major and said, "Could I trouble you for the sugar, old boy?"

"No trouble at all," the Sergeant Major said to Chin-

gachgook, and then turned to the Bugle Boy and said
softly, "Awfully civilized chaps, these Mohicans."

"We were speaking of the Fort, I believe, perfectly awful place," Robin said.

"Why?" asked the Bugle Boy. He was beginning to get
perturbed with Robin and Chingachgook. With these two
there was simply too much tea and not enough adventure.

"Well," Robin said, "first of all it's dark and dank and
musty."

"Terribly musty," Chingachgook put in.

"And Chingachgook has allergies."

"They're quite awful this time of year," Chingachgook
said, and the Sergeant Major clicked his tongue sympa-
thetically.

"And the decor," said Robin, throwing his hands up in
the air in disgust. "Simply not to be believed. And of
course the place is a frightful mess."

"They never think of cleaning," Chingachgook said
disapprovingly.

"No indeed," said Robin, "I can think of far nicer
places than the Fort."

"Yes," said Chingachgook, "the window boxes can be
lovely this time of year, and of course the garden!"

"Well, the garden is charming," said Robin, and the
two of them smiled most pleasantly at their guests.

"Really," said the Sergeant Major. "And there aren't
any cats in the garden, I shouldn't think, eh?" he said
hopefully.

"In the garden?" asked Robin incredulously.

"Don't be ridiculous," said Chingachgook, as if such a thing were unheard of.

"Well," said the Sergeant Major, "I for one am for popping off to the garden then."

The Bugle Boy and Perseus were fit to be tied.

"I can't believe you guys!" exclaimed the Bugle Boy.

" 'The garden can be lovely!' " mocked Perseus in disgust.

"Well, it can," Robin said defensively.

" 'Chingachgook has allergies!' " the Bugle Boy said, mimicking the Indian chieftain.

"They can be quite unpleasant!" Chingachgook replied. "Most unpleasant, actually."

Perseus and the Bugle Boy looked at each other in amazement.

"What kind of heroes are you guys anyway?" the Bugle Boy blurted out.

Robin Hood looked shocked by the question. He drew himself up quite stiffly and in a most dignified manner replied, "Why, British heroes, of course!"

"Hear! hear!" said the Sergeant Major approvingly.

"Well said, Hood," Chingachgook said to his friend.

"Don't you all understand what's at stake here?" asked Perseus incredulously.

"What?" Robin asked in a challenging tone of voice.

"The Little Boy!" said the Bugle Boy.

"Little Boy?" said Robin, looking about.

"Little Boy?" Chingachgook repeated in the same tone of voice.

"My dear fellow," said Robin, "this is the attic. There are no little boys in the attic!"

"There is a little boy in the nursery," Perseus said.

"And that's just where he belongs," said Robin.

"This chap makes perfect sense," the Sergeant Major declared.

The Little Bugle Boy's head was spinning. These fellows simply wouldn't understand.

Perseus and the Bugle Boy looked at one another and then all of a sudden Perseus understood it all quite clearly.

"Look," he said, "do you remember when you said that something strange had happened, something like being put under a spell like in the story of Sleeping Beauty?"

"Yes," answered Robin.

"Well, that was when the Little Boy whom you remember grew up to be a man and no longer believed in you. Without a child to believe in you . . . in any of us . . . none of us is real. So that was the time when you thought you were under a spell. Then *our* Little Boy came along, and he *does* believe in toys."

"He certainly does!" said the Bugle Boy.

"So that made us real again! That made you real again, too, because his father must have told him about you. But now he's sick and if the Little Boy dies . . . there will be no one to believe in us. Without a child to believe in us, we'll all die as well."

"Oh dear," said Robin.

"Oh dear indeed," said Chingachgook.

"That's why we have to find Davin, because the Little Boy believes that Davin has the power to make sick children well again," the Bugle Boy said.

"Well," said Robin, "I do seem to remember a story about Davin . . . that he had the power . . ."

"Hood," said Chingachgook, "if they're right . . ."

"Yes, well," said Robin, "if they're right that does put a different light on things. What do you say, Ching," said Robin, who had a habit of calling Chingachgook Ching for short, "shall we give it a go then?"

"Splendid idea, Hood!" said the last of the Mohicans.

So without any further argument, except the mutterings of the Sergeant Major, who begged them to consider going off on holiday to the garden, Perseus, the Bugle Boy, Robin Hood and his friend Chingachgook, and after much coaxing and persuading, the Sergeant Major, too, set off across the great dark open spaces of the attic toward the Fort.

14

Into the Darkness

"Awfully dark here," said the Little Bugle Boy.

"Yes, I'd love a dark beer," said the Sergeant Major.

"No," said Perseus, "he said it's awfully dark here."

"Who said?" asked the Sergeant Major.

"The Little Bugle Boy," said Perseus.

"What *about* him?" asked the Sergeant Major, who was growing more and more frustrated with the conversation.

" 'Dark here,' " Perseus all but shouted, "he said . . . 'dark here.' "

"The Little Bugle Boy said that?" the Sergeant Major asked.

"Yes," said Perseus.

"Out of the question!" snorted the Sergeant Major.

"What's out of the question?" the Bugle Boy asked.

"You're much too young for dark beer and I won't hear any more talk of it at all."

The Bugle Boy and Perseus gave up trying to tell the Sergeant Major that it was dark there in the attic. The truth was that the Sergeant Major was not just hard of hearing. He was slightly deaf, all right, but that was not at all the problem. The problem was that right now he was very very much afraid. He was so frightened in fact that he was having considerable difficulty concentrating on anything besides putting one foot in front of the other. And one of the reasons that he was so frightened was because it was so dark.

"It *is* awfully dark here," the Little Bugle Boy thought. The attic was darker by far than the Little Boy's room. It was darker than the shoe box had been. It was darker than lying in the folds of the Little Boy's blue blanket. It was darker even than being held in Aldo's mouth when the sheepdog had picked the Bugle Boy and the Sergeant Major up off the carpet and carried them back down the hall to the Little Boy's room. Though of course it wasn't nearly as sticky and gooey and slobbery as being in Aldo the sheepdog's mouth. Still, it was darker.

And when there was a teeny glimmer of light or just enough eerie glow from something shining in the darkness to be able to see at all, what you *could* see was so scary that it almost made you wish you *couldn't* see. It seemed as if everything had eyes that followed their every movement across the attic floor. Red glowing rat eyes shining in the dark followed them and then disappeared once again. Two old bookends lay in a corner with monsters on them, short little monsters sitting on their haunches like the kind that sat on the roof of the Cathedral of Notre Dame in Paris, as Robin Hood had explained when the Little Bugle Boy pointed them out.

"Paris, Shmaris," the Little Bugle Boy thought, "they're still monsters."

And then there were bugs.

Huge cockroaches scurried across the attic floor like hard-shelled rats with antennae twitching this way and that. One bumped right into the Bugle Boy and the boy all but jumped out of his skin.

A giant black water beetle waddled out of the shadows, passed the Little Bugle Boy and looked back as if to say What are you doing in the attic, young fool?

And that was when the Little Bugle Boy hit the web.

It was so dark he hadn't noticed it until he'd run into it. Then, once he had run into it, he didn't know what it was until it was too late. Thin lines like rope or string strung out in front of him. They stretched as he walked into them as if they would break from the force of his weight, but they didn't break. The strings were in fact very very strong and very very sticky, so sticky that he was stuck. Stuck like glue. Stuck like a rat in a trap or a fly on a frog's tongue or a bug in a—

Suddenly the thought dawned on him that he was stuck in a web . . . a spider's web. His eyes focused in the darkness and he looked over his right shoulder and saw one of the most ghastly sights he had ever seen in his entire, though admittedly short, life. Stuck to the web over his left shoulder was a poor pitiful moth wrapped in a sticky silky cocoon that held it prisoner there in the web like a sticky silky coffin in a sticky silky grave in a sticky silky graveyard full of rotting corpses that something planned to eat and, in this case, that something was coming down the web right now.

The Bugle Boy felt it before he saw it. He felt the web begin to vibrate, to tremble with the weight of something new coming toward him, coming down to get him. He looked up and there was the spider . . . coming down to eat *him*!

15

The Spider

The Bugle Boy remembered about spiders. He remembered that the family sang about them in the Little Boy's nursery rhymes.

" 'Oh the eensie weensie spi-der went up the water-spout,' " the boy and his parents would sing, as if spiders in general or, more to the point, this spider in particular were something cute to sing about.

This particular spider was not so eensie weensie. This spider was more like bigsie ugly! Andre Arachnid danced down the web on his crooked stick legs and swung out over the Little Bugle Boy on a single strand of web that he spewed out of his spinnerets. The spider attached himself to the line like a mountain climber dangling off a cliff and lowered himself until he was directly over the Bugle Boy. The Bugle Boy felt the sticky strand that shot out of the spider's abdominal spinnerets loop around him like a boa constrictor. Andre circled his strand around the Bugle Boy as if the Little Bugle Boy were a wayward calf and the spider a master cowboy. This was not, however, some cowpoke throwing a single loop around a steer. These strands the spider spun and circled around the Little Bugle Boy encased him like a mummy, wrapping him quickly in silky sticky ropes that bound his hands to his body and promised to turn him into the same kind of cocoon that held the dead moth captive in the spider's web.

The Little Bugle Boy opened his mouth to scream, but before any sound could escape his lips, the spider, as if realizing that the Little Bugle Boy was calling out to his friends, looped a strand around his mouth and then another, gagging him, stifling the Little Bugle Boy's cry for help.

"I say, Hood," said Chingachgook.

"What?" replied Robin.

"Did you hear anything?"

"No," said Robin, "did you?"

"Did I what?" the Sergeant Major said, as if waking from a deep sleep.

"Did you hear anything?" repeated Robin Hood.

"Why," said the Sergeant Major, "did you say something?"

"*I* did!" said Perseus.

"You said something?" asked the Sergeant Major.

"No, I *heard* something," said Perseus, turning around and peering into the darkness.

"I could have sworn I did, too, actually," said Chingachgook.

"Really," said Robin. "What did it sound like?"

"Well," said Chingachgook, "I can't be sure, of course, but I thought it was something like . . . *Haaaaaaaaaaaammmmmmpppppphhhh!*"

" 'Hummph,' " said the Sergeant Major. "I didn't hear anyone say 'hummph.' Why on earth would anyone say 'hummph'?"

"He didn't say 'hummph,' you twit," Perseus said.

" 'Twit'? Did you just call me a twit, you young scamp?" sputtered the Blustery Sergeant Major.

"He didn't say 'hummph,' he said—"

At that moment the Little Bugle Boy managed to slip the silky strand off his mouth and yell again, *"Hhhheeeeel-lllllppppp!"*

"I say," said Chingachgook, "there it is again. How very odd."

"Look!" said Perseus. He pointed off into the darkness where they could just make out the huge spider swinging slowly back and forth above the Little Bugle Boy, encasing him in his silky cocoon.

"Hol' on, little *amigo*. I'n comeen' to help ju," a new voice called out in a very heavy Spanish accent.

Perseus saw an old man dressed head to toe in black emerge from the darkness. The man wore black boots, a black shirt, black pants, a black mask and a black bandanna tied around his head. In one hand he held a long black bullwhip and in the other a sword.

"I say," said Chingachgook in amazement.

"Yes, there's a happy coincidence," said Robin Hood. "Just the man we've come to find."

"You mean," said Perseus, "that's—"

"El Lobo!" Robin said.

El Lobo lashed out with the bullwhip and looped the end of it around an old strand of web that stretched above the captive Little Bugle Boy. He didn't look any too sure of himself. He looked in fact as if it had been a long long time since he'd swung on a bullwhip. But then they say it's like riding a bicycle. Once you learn, you never forget.

He pulled against the bullwhip to make sure it would hold his weight and then, like a shaky trapeze artist, holding the bullwhip handle in one hand and the sword in the other, he swung across to the Little Bugle Boy.

"I think," said Robin, "he's swinging a bit too hard."

"Ummm . . . yes," said Chingachgook, watching El Lobo sailing through the air toward the spiderweb. "He does seem to have put a bit too much push into it, doesn't he? Of course," added the Mohican chieftain, "I suppose it all depends upon the landing."

"Yes, of course," Robin agreed.

"Whoa!" El Lobo shouted to no one in particular, and then, "Whoooooaaaaahhhhh *¡carramba!*"

So saying, or rather so shouting, the great El Lobo flew, arms and legs outstretched wide, spread-eagle, into the spiderweb. He stuck there like a fly swatted onto a wall. The only thing he could move freely was his wrist. That enabled him to swing his sword back and forth in a range

of not more than six inches. If the spider was foolish
enough to enter what El Lobo would later call "the six-
inch circle of death," he would be in terrible jeopardy. On
the other hand, if Andre Arachnid, the spider, did not
enter El Lobo's deadly circle, then the Little Bugle Boy
would be just an appetizer and El Lobo the main course.

Andre swung back and forth, first over El Lobo where
he was stuck on the web and then back over the Little
Bugle Boy. Andre tried to decide whether to finish the
cocoon he had started with the Little Bugle Boy, to start a
larger cocoon with the great El Lobo, or to eat one or
both, or a bit of each, or to do it now or later. "Decisions,
decisions, decisions," Andre thought.

And as he was thinking about which course to serve at
his dinner for one, two arrows flew through the air
straight at him.

The Little Bugle Boy looked up. Thank goodness for
Robin and Chingachgook! "I'm safe!"

At that very moment, however, the spider saw the arrows swooshing toward him and instead of being
skewered like a spider shish kebab, he slid down the silky
strand, gliding swiftly like a climber rapelling down a
mountainside. The arrows missed completely and Andre
thought, *"Dinner is served."* He hoisted himself back up
and prepared to feast upon the Little Bugle Boy, whom he
thought of now as the catch of the day.

16

Dinner with Andre

Perseus raced to the base of the web and pulled out his sword and hacked through the first strand, then the second, and then the third until he had cut through the bottom strands of webbing, which led up to the Bugle Boy's foot. He hoisted himself up next to the Bugle Boy, leaning back into the web with his left arm and hip. His right arm holding his sword remained free, and with it he began cutting through the cocoon that encased his little friend.

The spider began sliding down straight toward them, ready to inject them both with his venom. Perseus found there was nothing he could do now that his left arm and hip were stuck to the web. At the very last second, as the spider slid down to land on top of him, he thrust his sword up high, the point touching the spider's stomach.

The spider halted his descent and peered down at Perseus. He let out his high-pitched spider screech. Perseus held firm, the point of his sword pressed up against the spider's abdomen.

"Hmmmm," the spider thought, "perhaps I'll start the meal with a Spanish dish instead." He zipped up the strand from which he was hanging and swung toward El Lobo.

"*Venga!*" cried El Lobo. "Come, *Señor* Spider, if you want to fight like a man, step within my six-inch circle of death."

Andre did not want to fight like a man. He wanted to eat like a spider, and so he carefully avoided the six-inch circle in which El Lobo swung his sword.

Thhhuuunnnnggg! went Robin's bow.

Thhuuunnnnggg! went the bow of Chingachgook.

This time the arrows were aimed not at the spider, but at the two main strands that held the web in which El Lobo was a captive. Both arrows hit their marks, cutting through the two strands that held the web in place. Without these strands, El Lobo's weight was enough to do the rest.

"*Aaaaaaayyyyyyyyyy!*" screamed El Lobo as he went crashing down facefirst onto the floor.

This gave Perseus the time he needed and he hacked furiously with his sword at the spider's web. He cut through the strands that held what Andre the spider had started to think of as his Bugle Boy sandwich. The Little Bugle Boy would soon be free. Only one more strand held the cocoon in place. Perseus looked up and saw the spider flexing his eight long black legs. Andre was making a grabbing motion with them and it was clear that he planned to swoop down and grab the cocoon that held the Little Bugle Boy and then swing back up and out of harm's way, where he could eat the boy peacefully. Andre started to lower himself and Perseus knew he didn't have a moment to lose. He reared back with his sword and swung with all his might at the final strand that held the cocoon in place. With one mighty blow he cut through the silken line. The Bugle Boy, bound like a mummy, crashed to the floor. Perseus let out a triumphant cry.

Then he felt the eight legs grab him clawlike around his middle and start to pull *him* up toward the spider's stomach!

Seeing his friend in distress, Robin drew back his bow, and Thunnnngggg! Robin's arrow flew straight and true and cut through the line on which the spider dangled. The spider and Perseus tumbled through the darkness, falling to the floor below.

Perseus hit first, the spider landing right on top of him. Perseus rolled to his right and then to his left, struggling to get out from under the eight incredibly powerful legs that held him prisoner in their cage. He could find no escape.

"So, we meet again, eh, *señor?*" said El Lobo. "Now you will taste the blade of El Lobo." He stood, brandishing his sword, and in one swift move, thrust forward at Andre the spider.

Andre saw the sword point coming and crawled to his

right, giving Perseus just enough time to slide out from under him.

The spider lashed out with his front two legs, trying to catch El Lobo by the back of the neck and bring him in to his poisonous fangs.

"Aha! Two against one!" said El Lobo as the two legs lashed out at him. He parried each thrust of the spider's, slashing back and forth with his saber as if dueling with two swordsmen. The truth was El Lobo could no longer see as well as he used to and he believed he was facing two foes.

"As far as I an' concerned, ju are no spider . . . ju are nothing but a cockroach! Do you hear that, *cucaracha?* Your father was a stinkbug and your mother was a dung beetle. And now you will die like a pig at the hands of El Lobo."

He dodged the spider's thrust and lunged forward with his own blade. Robin and Chingachgook ran to his side, nocked fresh arrows in their bows and took careful aim at the spider.

When El Lobo saw them, he whirled upon the two of them. "What can ju be theenkin' of?" he demanded of Robin and Chingachgook. "This is a matter of honor," he said, *"mano a mano.* Or . . . *mano a* spider. Leave this eight-legged cockroach to El Lobo."

The problem of course was that in saying that to Chingachgook and Robin, he had turned his back on the spider, who now reached out with his front two legs and grabbed the masked Spaniard around the middle, forced him to the ground and began pulling him in toward his poisonous fangs.

"Don't just stand there!" shouted El Lobo to Robin and Chingachgook. "Do sometheen!"

"But you just said it was a matter of honor," said Robin unflappably.

"Well, now I'm sayin' that eet ees a matter of pain!" El Lobo cried.

"And," said Chingachgook, "you specifically told us to leave that cockroach to El Lobo!"

"Oh, please leave me to El Lobo," thought Andre the spider, and he lowered his fangs toward the back of the Spaniard's neck.

"Well, now I'm telling you *don't* leave the spider to El Lobo because El Lobo ees about to be eaten by the great big ugly hairy-legged spider!"

"Oh," said Robin Hood, suddenly understanding.

"Well," said Chingachgook, "I suppose that is different."

So saying, Chingachgook pulled his tomahawk from his belt and swung it down full force into Andre's right front leg.

"Ouch ooch ouch oooch eeeeech!" thought Andre, hopping about on seven spindly legs.

Whack! went the Mohican's tomahawk into yet another of Andre's appendages.

"Ooooch oooooch ooooooch oooooch!" Andre thought, hopping on six legs.

Whack! Thwack! Thunk! Chingachgook thrashed

about like a weed-whacking gardener whacking weeds, although in this case he was not a weed-whacking gardener but a knee-whacking Mohican.

Andre let loose of the Spaniard and hopped about on the only four legs he had that were not throbbing with pain.

Chingachgook took a deep breath, as if he were about to let out a ferocious Indian war whoop. Instead, he shouted something which under the circumstances was much more effective. "Shooooo!" he shouted with a very British accent. "Shooooooo, you nasty thing!"

Whereupon, Andre Arachnid hobbled off into the darkness, four knees aching, and considered whether or not it might be wiser and certainly less painful to become a vegetarian.

El Lobo painfully straightened himself up, looked at Chingachgook and Robin and said, "Ju have saved my life. I am at jour service. Ask anything that ju will of me . . . and I will not refuse."

"Very well," said the Sergeant Major, who had been hiding all this time inside a broken porcelain mermaid. "Since my friends and I have saved your life, show us the way to the Shelves and then to Davin."

17

To the Shelves!

"I think this story is getting too violent," said Grandma Goddess, and she closed the book.

"No!" said Yoni.

"No what?" said Grandma Goddess, taking off her reading glasses and folding them in her lap.

Yoni thought for a moment and then looked at her with his beautiful big velvety brown eyes and said sweetly, "No please?"

Grandma Goddess chuckled to herself and said, "That's not what I meant."

"Grandma Goddess," Adam said, leaning forward. "It's not getting too violent, honest. It's just kind of exciting, that's all."

"Yes," said Danielle. "The only thing wrong with it is there aren't any girls."

Grandma Goddess looked from one child to the other.

"You're sure it's not too violent?" she asked. "I don't want you to have nightmares because of some silly story."

"We won't have nightmares," Danielle protested.

"I don't know," Grandma Goddess said, shaking her head. "Spiders and tomahawks and arrows thwacking and thwunking."

"At least the spider didn't eat them," said Adam reasonably.

"And the thwacking and thwunking was just Chingachgook hitting Andre in the knees," said Yoni.

"Please," said Danielle.

Grandma Goddess looked at Danielle and said, "I thought there weren't enough girls in it for you."

"Well," said Danielle, "there weren't, but I'm sure there will be . . . won't there?"

"Well," said Grandma Goddess, "let's see." And she put her reading glasses back on, opened the book and began to read.

El Lobo took them to the Fort. It was a wild and woolly place, a world of broken and discarded toys of every description. There were Cowboys and Indians and alligators and frogs and golliwogs, there were Knights and soldiers and horses and pigs, all kinds of critters and even a live cockroach or two. They walked through the tumbledown gate of the Lincoln Logs Fort and stepped past the animal cracker box full of ferocious and moldy lion cookies. They walked past the well and the old Civil War cannon and the Roman catapult and headed for the saloon.

Once inside the saloon, the Sergeant Major, Perseus, Robin, Chingachgook and El Lobo took seats at the bar. They sat next to some of the wildest-looking desperadoes anyone had ever seen. There were Cowboys whose arms hung down connected to their torsos by rubber bands. There were circus performers in tights and tough-looking Russian hunters in long woolly coats with rifles as tall as they were themselves.

There on the bar El Lobo sketched for them a map that showed the way to that far-off place called the Shelves. At the very mention of the Shelves, the other patrons in the bar backed away and showed El Lobo and his friends a new measure of respect. No one had ever been to the Shelves—at least no one had ever been there and returned to tell the tale.

As they were planning the best route to take, a sudden flash of light illuminated not only the entire world of the attic, but also the gargoyle on the building across the way, which they saw through the skylight for an instant.

"El Diablo," said El Lobo.

"El Whatto?" asked the Blustery Sergeant Major.

"Eet ees *El Diablo,*" El Lobo said, pointing through the skylight at the gargoyle. "The Devil," he said.

"Don't be absurd, man," said the Blustery Sergeant Major. "It's nothing but a stone statue . . . nothing more and nothing less."

At that moment, the earth trembled beneath them. Explosions were blowing up outside their little world, out in the darkness far far away.

"And what about that, *señors*?" asked El Lobo.

"What do you think it is?" said Perseus.

"Eet ees *El Diablo*."

"No it isn't," said the Little Bugle Boy. "That's artillery or bombs being dropped." The Little Boy knew all about those things. "It's a war."

"A war . . . ," said El Lobo. "But they are people. They are supposed to know better. That is why I think it can only be . . . *El Diablo*."

"Yes," said Robin, "well, be that as it may, the problem that we face is not *El Diablo,* but how we get to the top of the Shelves. If we have to climb, it'll take us at least a week."

"That's right, Hood," said Chingachgook. "And from what our young friend has said, I'm afraid we don't have that long, as the Little Boy is very ill."

"And quite frankly," Robin said to El Lobo, "at your age, *señor,* I very much doubt that you could make it."

"At my age?" said El Lobo. "Look at theeese, my own teeth, my own hair. My veins burn with the fiery blood of a young man ready for adventure. *¡Tengo el fuego en mi sangre!* I am the Prince of *Peligro*! I am El Lobo!"

"Yes, well, I'm afraid it will take more than teeth, hair, and a plethora of nicknames to climb the Shelves, *señor,*" Robin replied.

El Lobo thought for a while and then looked up. Behind his mask they could see a gleam in his eye. "There ees one way," he said.

"Don't be a tease," said Robin.

"Yes," said the Blustery Sergeant Major, "if there's a way, tell us . . . as long as it doesn't involve the Nanny's cat."

El Lobo smiled and then said, "The plane."

The old aeroplane was a fantastic-looking thing, with dragonfly wings that they could see jutting out beneath a great veil of cobwebs. The wings were delicate-looking, with veinlike lines running through them. They were long and silvery and the cobwebs hung over them like moss hanging down from jungle trees.

"Cobwebs!" exclaimed the Blustery Sergeant Major. "Wouldn't you say that cobwebs are generally a good indication of the presence of . . . spiders! Haven't we had enough of spiders for one day, gentlemen?"

The masked Spaniard explained that these were very old cobwebs and the spiders lived in them no longer. He and Perseus hacked through the massive silken webbing with their swords as Chingachgook sneezed from his allergies.

"Oh dear," said Chingachgook, "you're raising an awful lot of dust, you know."

"I'm very sorry, *señor*," said El Lobo. "Next time you must tell the spiders to be neater, eh?"

Finally they had swept aside the cobwebs and the dust, the snail trails and rodent droppings, and revealed a magnificent dragon-winged double-cockpitted pre–World War I biplane.

It had a rubber-band engine with a propeller that could

be wound and wound and wound some more, until the
rubber band was one great twisted mass waiting to be
sprung. There was a lever in the rear cockpit that one
pushed forward to hold the propeller in place. When the
lever was pulled back, the propeller would spin furiously
and the plane would be airborne.

"Thees old dog will show you a new trick. Thees ees
the way we will get up to the top of the Shelves, *amigos!*"
exclaimed El Lobo.

◆ ◆ ◆ ◆ ◆ 18 ◆ ◆ ◆ ◆ ◆

The Pirate Ship

Perseus, El Lobo, and the Blustery Sergeant Major pushed on one of the wings while Robin, Chingachgook and the Little Bugle Boy pushed on the other. Slowly they wheeled the dragon-winged biplane out of its resting place and into the middle of the attic floor. The Little Bugle Boy looked up and saw it for the first time. Far off in the distance, stretching up and up and up, seemingly forever, were the Shelves. On the topmost shelf the Little Bugle Boy could just make out the outline of the Pirate Ship, and what looked like a huge man in a long flowing cape, and next to him was what appeared to be a young girl . . . They had found the Dark Knight and Princess Helen!

"Finally," said Danielle, "a girl."

"Shhh," said Yoni.

"Don't shush your cousin," said Grandma Goddess.

She looked down, found her place and continued to read,
glancing at Danielle with a wink and a smile. "I'm glad
there's finally a girl back in the story, too," she said.

High, high up on the very topmost shelf at the highest
point in the entire attic was the Pirate Ship. Next to it was
the shoe box full of toys, which had been foolishly placed
there by the Nanny. A wild celebration was in progress
on the Pirate Ship. Blackbeard's men shouted and ca-
roused, laughed and drank rum with the Dark Knight's
minions; with headless cavalrymen and the Dark Knight's
archers, with his soldiers and with his horsemen.

The Pirates shouted out, "Yo ho ho," and "Aaaaaarh,"
and "Aaaaaaaarh, matey!" and one sang out, " 'And I'm
never, ever sick at sea.' "

" 'What, never?' " Blackbeard's men sang in answer.

" 'No, never!' " they replied, dancing about the deck of
the ship.

They were very fierce-looking pirates indeed and there
was no doubt at all that none of them ever washed up
before eating. As far as their teeth were concerned, it went
without saying that all of Blackbeard the Pirate's men had
very poor dental hygiene.

Princess Helen stood with her hands bound behind her
back and a blindfold across her eyes. "Where are you
taking me?" she boldly demanded.

"Aaaaaarh," said Blackbeard. "Ye will soon see where
we be taking ye, lass."

"I'll see a lot better without this blindfold," said Princess Helen.

"Aaaaarh," Blackbeard said scornfully. "A saucy lass, no less."

"All in good time, Your Highness," said the Dark Knight, his deep bass voice booming. "All in good time."

Princess Helen tried to shrug off the Dark Knight's hand as he grabbed her by the shoulder. "I'm not going a step farther!" she said with great defiance.

"Oh, I think you will, Your Highness," said the Dark Knight, putting his sword against her back, "if . . . you get my point."

"Aaaaaarh," said Blackbeard. "And if ye do not step lively, ye will assuredly get his point," he said, and laughed.

The Dark Knight pushed Princess Helen forward at swordpoint.

"Is that the Princess?" Perseus asked, pointing up at the Pirate Ship. His voice trembled.

Perseus, El Lobo, the Bugle Boy, the Blustery Sergeant Major, Robin Hood, and Chingachgook watched in horror as a plank was pushed off the bow of the Pirate Ship, protruding out over the edge of that fearsome vessel, which flew the skull and crossbones from its topmost mast. The Dark Knight put his sword to Princess Helen's back and made her step forward onto the plank, walking to its very edge.

One more step and she would tumble off the plank. Down below, the heroes watched, holding their breaths.

"He'll never push her off," the Blustery Sergeant Major

proclaimed. "It's just a bluff, that's all, just the bluff of a bully."

Unfortunately, the Blustery Sergeant Major was wrong, and the Dark Knight pushed his sword between Princess Helen's shoulder blades so that she was forced to step one step farther, and with that step, she tumbled off the gangplank, falling through the darkness toward certain destruction.

"Grandma Goddess!" said Danielle, obviously very distressed.

"What, my sweet girl?" said Grandma Goddess.

"Grandma Goddess," Danielle said again, as worried as before, "that *can't* be right!"

"What can't be right?" asked Grandma Goddess.

"That part about . . . well, Princess Helen can't fall off the gangplank to certain destruction! You must have read that wrong."

"Do you think so?" asked Grandma Goddess.

"Yes!" said Danielle.

"Hmmmmm," said Grandma Goddess, and her finger traced back up the page until she found the words that she had read. "No," she said, "that's just exactly what it says . . . she tumbled off the gangplank, falling through the darkness toward certain destruction."

"But that's terrible!" protested Danielle.

"Well then," said Grandma Goddess, "maybe I should stop reading."

"No!" all three children said at once.

"All right," said Grandma Goddess, "if you're sure . . ."

"We're sure," Adam said.

So Grandma Goddess continued.

". . . she tumbled off the gangplank, falling through the darkness toward certain destruction. Princess Helen screamed as she fell through space and then, in midair, her fall was broken as the rope that was tied around her chest and under her arms snapped taut."

"Oohhh," said Danielle, "she had a rope around her! Whew!" she said. "Writers are really sneaky."

"Yes," Grandma Goddess agreed, "they certainly are."

Princess Helen dangled by the rope that hung over the edge of the gangplank, swinging back and forth in the darkness.

Her blindfold had slipped and the Princess beheld a terrifying sight as she hung high above the attic floor. It was as if she were dangling high above the Grand Canyon and the only thing that kept her from plunging to her death was the rope around her chest.

"Haul her up," said the Dark Knight to Blackbeard's men.

The Pirates pulled on the rope and slowly hoisted Princess Helen back up to the gangplank.

"Take her below and put her in irons. Let her think about what has just happened all night long. Have pleasant dreams, Your Highness," the Dark Knight said. "And tomorrow, we'll do it all once again."

"You fiend," Princess Helen said.

"Ha ha ha ha ha," laughed the Dark Knight cruelly. "Tomorrow you shall either tell us where Davin is or I will not only push you off the gangplank once again, but I will also cut the rope. And this time, Your Highness, I promise you there will be nothing to break your fall. Ha ha ha ha ha," he laughed.

"You're so easily amused," said Princess Helen. "But I'm not afraid. You can do whatever you want, but you'll never win. The Little Boy will be saved!"

"Then you, Your Worship, are a fool," said the Dark Knight angrily.

"Aaaaaaaarh," said Blackbeard the Pirate.

19

Airborne

"Heave!" said the Blustery Sergeant Major.
"Ho!" called Robin Hood.

"Heave!" said the Blustery Sergeant Major once again. Perseus, El Lobo and the Sergeant Major pulled down on one end of the rickety old propeller of the dragon-winged double-cockpitted biplane as Robin and Chingachgook pushed up against the other side of the same propeller. Working together, they were able to turn the propeller one full revolution and twist the rubber-band motor one notch tighter.

"Heave!" said the Blustery Sergeant Major.

"Ho!" answered Robin Hood.

The Sergeant Major, Perseus and El Lobo pulled, Robin and Chingachgook pushed, and with each push and pull, each full turn of the propeller, the Little Bugle Boy, who sat in the rear cockpit, yanked the lever back to allow the propeller and its rubber-band motor to be wound another notch. While the others caught their breaths and got ready to crank the propeller again, the Bugle Boy pushed the lever forward to hold the propeller in place.

The rubber band was twisted to the breaking point.

"I think that's quite enough," said the Blustery Sergeant Major.

"Well, old bean," said Chingachgook, "I think we really ought to try to give it one more for good measure. Better safe than sorry . . . that's what we Mohicans always say."

"Yes, well, my back is killing me," complained the Sergeant Major, "and that's what *I* have to say."

"Oh come come come," Robin Hood chided him. "Let's give it the old school try, eh, Sergeant Major?"

The poor Sergeant Major put his hands on his knees, caught his breath, then grabbed hold of the propeller and said, "Heave."

"Ho!" answered Robin Hood.

They heaved and ho'ed, pushed and pulled, sweated and strained and finally got the propeller to turn one extra notch.

"Good show!" said Chingachgook.

"Yes, well," said the Sergeant Major, "*bon voyage,* keep your powder dry, don't fire till you see the whites of their eyes and happy hunting. We'll be down here cheering you on."

You see the poor Blustery Sergeant Major was afraid of

many things, but he was afraid of nothing quite so much as he was afraid of flying. Flying and heights, heights and flying, they went hand in hand and he liked neither of them very much at all.

"But surely you're going with us," said Robin Hood to the Blustery Sergeant Major.

"There is absolutely nothing you can say that will make me get into that infernal contraption," said the Blustery Sergeant Major.

"Really?" said Perseus.

"Yes, really," said the Sergeant Major.

"The Nanny's tabby cat is coming," Perseus said, pointing at the tabby, who had pushed her way through the attic door and was beginning to pad toward them.

"I'll sit in front," said the Sergeant Major.

And with surprising alacrity and grace for a man of his age and girth, the Sergeant Major grabbed hold of the strut, put his foot on the wheel housing and hauled himself up onto the fantastic dragon-shaped wing of the aeroplane. From there he dove headfirst into the front cockpit, leaving two stubby legs kicking out into the air.

Robin and Chingachgook quickly righted the Sergeant Major. Perseus climbed in to share the front cockpit with him, while the Bugle Boy and El Lobo shared the rear cockpit, as El Lobo *was* the only one of them who knew how to fly a plane.

Robin and Chingachgook stood one on each wing holding on to the struts as the Nanny's cat drew closer and closer, her purrrrrrrr filling the attic.

"Ready for takeoff?" asked El Lobo.

"More than ready," shouted the Sergeant Major, looking back over his shoulder in terror of the Nanny's cat.

"I wasn't asking you," said El Lobo. "I was talking to my copilot," he said, indicating the Little Bugle Boy.

The cat looked up, recognized the Sergeant Major and licked her chops.

"Yes, well, I'm talking to you!" shouted the Sergeant Major. "Take off!"

"All right, *amigos*," said El Lobo. He looked at the Little Bugle Boy and said, "Contact!"

"Contact!" replied the Little Bugle Boy. He pulled back with all his might on the lever and let it go just as the Nanny's tabby cat sprang at them out of the darkness.

The biplane shuddered, the propeller spun, and the plane edged forward down the length of the attic floor as the Nanny's tabby landed, missing them by a whisker.

"Tally ho!" shouted Chingachgook as the plane leaped into the air.

The Nanny's cat stood on her hind legs and clawed the air, watching the plane soar over her head. The Sergeant Major scowled down at the cat, stuck out his tongue and blew raspberries, laughing until he looked up and realized that he was in an airplane flying up and up and up.

"Whhhhooooooooaaaaaooooooooo!" he shouted at the top of his lungs.

"Yes, yes," shouted Robin, smiling, "that's the spirit! Jolly good fun, eh?"

The biplane sailed through the attic air, drawing closer

and closer to the Shelves. The plan called for them to land on the second-highest shelf, rescue Princess Helen from the ship, then make their escape in the plane.

El Lobo brought the plane in for a pass by the shelf, only to see that it was full of rusted old gardening tools.

Hoes and jagged rake heads, hand shovels, trowels and pitchforklike tools were scattered across the length of the shelf so that there was no possible way of landing. To avoid being skewered by a rake head, El Lobo had to throw the plane into a steep bank to the right, almost pitching the Sergeant Major from the cockpit.

"Land this plane immediately, you madman!" bellowed the Sergeant Major.

Unfortunately, the only place to land was the third shelf from the top. The plane scooted in among bins of bobby pins and buttons, scraps of fabric and giant cushions punched through with sewing needles. The plane skidded and slid to the very edge of the shelf, so that it looked as if it might go over the side before finally coming to rest next to an unraveled dressmaker's measuring tape.

"Maniac!" the Sergeant Major shouted, hitting El Lobo in the head with his hat.

The rescue party climbed from the biplane and set about the business at hand.

Robin, Chingachgook, and El Lobo would climb up to the Pirate Ship to rescue Princess Helen while Perseus, the Sergeant Major and the Bugle Boy stood watch over the plane. Perseus was furious that he was not to be included in the rescue party, especially when El Lobo said, "Thees is the work of a man, not a boy."

"I can handle a sword as well as you," said Perseus, and to prove it he drew his blade on El Lobo.

"Now, now," said Robin, "no one doubts your abilities, but it just makes good sense to have someone in reserve, especially someone as obviously handy with a blade as yourself."

"Quite so, quite so," said the Blustery Sergeant Major, "sound tactics, very regimental and all that, eh?"

Perseus sulked, muttering that he had come all this way to have adventures and rescue the Princess. However, he realized that Robin was the most experienced of the group and since he was in charge, Perseus decided he would follow the plan and guard the plane. Leaving the Sergeant Major, the Bugle Boy and Perseus behind, Robin, Chingachgook and El Lobo set off for the Pirate Ship on their quest to rescue Princess Helen.

Little did they know that the Dark Knight and his men had seen them . . . and were waiting.

◆ ◆ ◆ ◆ 20 ◆ ◆ ◆ ◆

The Rescue

As they crept silently up toward the Pirate Ship, Robin, Chingachgook and El Lobo could hear the Pirates singing drunkenly.

" 'Poor Little Buttercup, sweet Little Buttercup . . . ,' " the drunken Pirates sang out of tune, although it must be said that they sang with great expression.

"I wonder if they know anything from *Pirates of Penzance,*" mused Robin.

The three heroes reached the anchor chain. Robin and Chingachgook slung their bows across their chests while El Lobo made sure that his sword would in no way interfere with the climbing. Hand over hand, the three men pulled themselves up the chain and over the gunwales and huddled in the shadows of the ship's bow.

"I should think they're holding her somewhere below deck," said Robin Hood.

"Yes," said Chingachgook. "The problem is, however, that the sight of a man in green tights, not to mention a black-masked Spaniard and a Mohican in a breechcloth, climbing about on a Pirate Ship may just draw undue attention."

"I hadn't thought of that, Ching," said Robin Hood, "but you might be right."

"Those three chaps look about the right size, wouldn't you say, Hood?" said Chingachgook.

"Indeed," said Robin Hood.

Three Pirates sat on a forward hatch, yo-ho-ho-ing and drinking their rum. They were a filthy, unseemly lot who were so absorbed in their singing and drinking that they did not notice Robin, Chingachgook and El Lobo sneaking up toward them in the shadows.

"Aaaaaaarh," said the First Pirate.

"Aye," said the Second Pirate agreeably.

"Ahem," said Robin Hood, clearing his throat and stepping up toward the Pirates.

"Aaaaaaarh," said the First Pirate.

"I say," said Robin, "you nautical types do seem to have quite a limited vocabulary."

"Who be ye?" demanded the First Pirate.

"I be . . . ," said Robin, trying to fall into the Pirates' rhythm, "I be . . . Hood, Robin Hood. And who, might I ask, do you be? Or, be you . . . or however you chaps would put it."

The First Pirate looked Robin up and down. He was obviously not much impressed by what he saw. He pulled out his dagger and said in a low and menacing growl, "I be he what's going to run ye through!"

"Oh dear," said Robin, "but then what's that?" So saying, he pointed down at the First Pirate's toes, wearing a look of shocked concern.

The Pirate looked down to where Robin was pointing, and what he saw was Robin's fist coming straight up in a wicked uppercut right into his jaw. The blow lifted the Pirate back up off his feet and he fell into a coil of rope.

The Second Pirate was reaching for the pistol hooked in his belt when he felt a tap on his shoulder. He turned to receive a ferocious head butt from Chingachgook.

The Third Pirate reached for his sword, drew it and pointed his blade at Robin.

"Swordplay?" asked Robin. "No," he said, "I think not. Now if it's bows and arrows, I'm your man. But if it's swords, I really think it's that chap you'll want to talk to."

The Pirate turned to where he supposed he would find a ready swordsman waiting to battle him to the death. What he saw, however, was nothing. El Lobo was not there. The masked Spaniard had climbed into the rigging and was perched on a boom holding a rope. When the Pirate looked up, El Lobo jumped off the boom, swinging on the rope. He was having so much fun he forgot entirely about his arthritis and bursitis and all his aches and pains. He flew through the air, heels first, until those very same heels smacked square into the jaw of the Third Pirate.

"Well done," said Robin Hood.

"I would have preferred," said El Lobo, "to duel with him with my sword. But then perhaps I would have ruined the shirt."

"Yes, well, that would have been a very great pity," said Chingachgook.

"Nothing like boarding a Pirate Ship to make a masked man feel young again," said El Lobo happily.

Chingachgook, Robin and El Lobo changed into the Pirates' clothes and left Blackbeard's men sitting in their underwear tied to the forward mast with gags in their mouths. The three heroes opened the forward hatch and crept down the stairway in search of Princess Helen.

The rescue party made its way stealthily down the stairs. Walking up toward them was a fierce-looking peg-legged Pirate.

"I say . . . ," said Robin politely.

Chingachgook poked Robin in the ribs.

"Oh yes," whispered Robin Hood to Chingachgook, "I forgot, of course." He looked to the peg-legged Pirate and said, "Uh . . . what I meant to say was . . . Aaaaaaaarh!"

"Aaaaaaarh!" growled the ferocious-looking peg-legged Pirate.

"Yes, aaaaaaaarh indeed," said Robin Hood. "I wonder

if you'd be good enough to tell me where the Princess is being held captive, Peg." And then he added thoughtfully, "May I call you Peg?"

The fierce-looking peg-legged Pirate quickly reached for his blunderbuss. To stop him, Robin instantly and quite viciously stomped on the peg-legged Pirate's one good foot.

Now, you know what you do when someone steps on your toe? You hop about on your other foot. Well, that is precisely what the ferocious-looking peg-legged Pirate tried to do.

Unfortunately for him, he was not very good at hopping about on his peg. In fact, he hopped so hard that his peg punctured a knothole and got stuck in the decking.

As he reached down to try and pull the peg up out of the deck, he found himself looking straight into El Lobo's sword point.

"You were about to tell us, *señor,* the whereabouts of the Princess?" said the Spanish swordsman.

Armed with the keys to the brig, which they had taken off the now bound and gagged, not to mention stuck in a knothole, peg-legged Pirate, Robin, Chingachgook and El Lobo made their way down the dark corridor to Princess Helen's cell. There they saw the Princess, chained to the back wall.

They unlocked the shackles and Princess Helen looked up defiantly and said, "Where do you think you're taking me, you filthy scum?"

"We're taking you to the Bugle Boy and to Davin. And for your information, *madame,* the name is not Scum. It's Hood."

"And not *filthy* Hood, either," said Chingachgook. "His name is Robin."

21

A Trap

"I don't know anyone named Hood or Robin," Princess Helen said impatiently, her eyes flashing with anger at the three men, who were looking around nervously while they tried to rush her out of her cell.

"*Señorita,* please," implored the Spaniard.

"I told you I don't know anyone named Hood," said Princess Helen.

"Not even the Red Riding?" asked El Lobo.

"Please, my dear," said Chingachgook, "you've really got to believe us."

"Why?" said Princess Helen, pulling her arm out of Chingachgook's grip. "How do I know this isn't a trap? How do I know you're not Blackbeard's men trying to trick me?"

"Honestly," said Robin, "do we look like Blackbeard's men?"

"Yes!" said Princess Helen.

"Hood," said Chingachgook, "She, uh . . . has a point." Chingachgook pointed at the Pirate clothes they were all wearing.

"Ah yes," said Robin Hood. "Well, there's a perfectly logical explanation for the clothes. We're in disguise."

"You're in dis-*guise*," Princess Helen said sarcastically.

"Yes," said Robin Hood. "If you must know, I usually wear these smashing green tights and a perky little plumed hat, set at a jaunty angle."

"As for me," said El Lobo, "I prefer something basic in black."

"I'm more a skin and bones man, myself," Chingachgook added.

Princess Helen was looking from one to the other as if she were trying to decide whether or not green was really a good color for Robin when Chingachgook interrupted her thoughts.

"See here, Your Highness, you told the Bugle Boy to find El Lobo, did you not?" he asked.

"Yes," said Princess Helen. "How did you know?"

"Well, who do you think *this* is?" Chingachgook said, pointing at the famous Spanish swordsman.

"He looks like a Pirate," Princess Helen said. She took a sniff and wrinkled her nose. "And he certainly smells like a Pirate, so for all I know—"

El Lobo cut Princess Helen off in the middle of her sentence and pulled his sword from its scabbard, extending it toward her face. Carved in ornate letters running down the length of the blade were the words THIS SWORD IS THE PROPERTY OF EL LOBO. IF FOUND, PLEASE RETURN TO EL LOBO, POSTAGE PAID, SIGNED EL LOBO.

Princess Helen read the words on the sword blade and looked up at the masked Spaniard.

"How do I know this sword is really yours?" she said suspiciously.

"Oh really," said Chingachgook, "this *is* getting to be a bit much!"

El Lobo raised a cautioning hand to the last of the Mohicans. "No," he said, "No, the lady is cautious. She is suspicious. I an sure she has her reasons."

"Well, I *have* been kidnapped, blindfolded, bound and gagged and forced to walk the plank," said Princess Helen, "and then dragged down here and chained to this wall!"

"Yes," said El Lobo, "those essperiences can certainly color your thinking, but perhaps this will set your mind at ease, *señorita.*" So saying, he rolled up his right sleeve and revealed a tattoo of a heart with the words EL LOBO LOVES MARIA CONSUELA.

Princess Helen looked at the tattoo and said, "Who is Maria Consuela?"

"No, *señorita,*" said El Lobo, "the point ees *not* who ees Maria Consuela, the point ees . . . *I* am El Lobo!"

"See?" said Robin. "Told you so."

"All right, all right," said Princess Helen, "but you can never be too careful. Anyway," she said, "thank goodness you're here."

"Apologies accepted," said Robin Hood. "Now I really do think it would be wise to leave."

Robin, Chingachgook, Princess Helen and El Lobo made their way through the corridor past the bound and gagged peg-legged Pirate and up the stairs to the forward hatch.

"Something's wrong," Robin whispered.

"What?" asked Princess Helen.

"I don't hear any more singing," said Robin. "It's too quiet. I don't like it."

"I didn't much care for their singing anyway," said Chingachgook.

"Mohicans can be such snobs," sniffed Robin. Slowly and carefully, he peeked over the edge of the forward hatch. There appeared to be no one on the deck of the Pirate Ship at all. He looked this way and that but saw no trace of the Pirates, the Dark Knight or his men.

"All right," Robin said, "let's go."

The three men and the Princess crept onto the deck and moved quickly toward the bow, where the anchor chain waited. Their plan was to climb back down the chain and make their way down the Shelves to the aeroplane. It was a good plan and it most assuredly should have worked.

"Leaving so soon, Your Highness?" boomed the voice of the Dark Knight. "Without even bothering to say good-bye?"

Robin, Chingachgook, El Lobo and Princess Helen

whirled around, and as they did, the Dark Knight slid down from the rigging on a rope behind them. From every corner Pirates and the Dark Knight's men snaked from underneath hatchways, threw off tarpaulins or jumped down from the rigging onto the deck. They were everywhere and they surrounded Princess Helen and the three who had come to rescue her.

"I knew they would send someone to rescue you," the Dark Knight said to Princess Helen, "but I never expected it would be the great Robin Hood himself!"

Robin turned to Princess Helen and said, "You see, *he* knows who I am." Robin turned back to the Dark Knight and said, "If I had my feathered cap I would take it off to you, sir, but since I seem to have misplaced it, this will have to do." In a lightning-quick move Robin whipped out the dagger he wore in his belt and slashed through the rope that was tied off at the mast next to him. The rope held the rigging suspended over the Dark Knight's head, and with the rope sliced neatly in two the rigging plummeted to the deck.

"Watch out!" yelled the Dark Knight, and he jumped out of the way and narrowly missed being crushed by the wood and canvas that crashed down from above.

Chingachgook and Robin unslung their bows. El Lobo unsheathed his sword and tossed Princess Helen his bullwhip. She cast an appreciative eye on the whip, tested its weight with a mighty *crack!* and the fight was on.

Robin and Chingachgook took aim and fired at the

tied-off lines that held the ship's sails above the foredeck.
The sails and ropes, beams and pulleys came crashing
down on the Pirates and the Dark Knight's men. El Lobo
dueled with four men at once while Princess Helen gave
three others a taste of the lash. The four heroes fought
their way valiantly into the bow of the ship.

"All right," said Robin to Princess Helen and El Lobo,
"you two go over the side first and slide down the anchor
chain and Chingachgook and I will hold them off and
then follow."

A Pirate blocked their way. El Lobo sent him sprawling
with a swift kick and he and Princess Helen went over the
side and down the anchor chain to the shelf. Robin and
Chingachgook fought like madmen, throwing the Pirates
back again and again until they could hold them off no
longer, and then they jumped over the side of the ship,
clinging to the anchor chain.

Nothing could have prepared them for what they now
saw. Princess Helen and El Lobo both had been bound
hand and foot and gagged by Blackbeard the Pirate and
the rest of his men.

"Aaaaaarh, that's right," growled Blackbeard, "it was *all*
a trap and ye've fallen right into it!"

He held his saber up to Princess Helen's throat, smiled
malevolently and said, "Now then, 'Ood, nice and
easy . . . down the chain or the Princess dies."

There was no choice but to do exactly as Blackbeard
said. Robin and Chingachgook slid gingerly down the

anchor chain and surrendered their weapons as the Dark Knight appeared above them, looking past the railing, gloating over the prisoners just taken.

"Now," said the Dark Knight, "I will know where Davin is or you *all* shall die."

22

Escape

Down below, Perseus, the Bugle Boy and the Blustery Sergeant Major watched in horror as their friends and Princess Helen were taken captive by the Dark Knight and Blackbeard the Pirate. They watched helplessly as the Dark Knight directed his men to tie up Robin, Chingachgook and El Lobo. The three of them were taken to the edge of the shelf and their hands were tied together. And then they saw the gangplank.

It was a huge plank of wood that stuck out over the edge of the topmost shelf. El Lobo, Chingachgook and Robin Hood were marched out onto the plank at swordpoint, their hands bound by a single rope.

Then Perseus, the Sergeant Major and the Bugle Boy gasped all together as they watched their three friends being pushed all at once off the gangplank. They dangled there, high above in midair, by a single rope that stretched over the gangplank and was the only thing that kept them from falling to a certain death.

"Where's Princess Helen?" whispered the Bugle Boy.

"Shhh," said Perseus.

Just then they saw a second gangplank being pushed out from the bow of the Pirate Ship so that it too was perched over the edge of the shelf. Onto this gangplank Princess Helen was now marched. The Dark Knight stood behind her, his sword at her back.

Blackbeard the Pirate marched onto the lower gangplank, from which Robin, Chingachgook and El Lobo were suspended. Blackbeard pulled his sword from its scabbard and let the blade brush back and forth against the rope that held the three heroes. As the sharp steel touched the rope, tiny fibers split beneath the razor-edged saber. With each set of fibers that was cut, the rope unraveled just a bit and strained ever more with the weight of the three captives.

"Take a good look, Your Highness," said the Dark Knight to Princess Helen. "The fate of your friends rests solely in your hands."

Perseus, the Bugle Boy and the Sergeant Major looked on as Robin, Chingachgook and El Lobo swung dangerously back and forth high above them. If the rope was cut, they would never survive that great fall to the floor below.

Perseus turned to the Bugle Boy and the Sergeant Major. "It's up to us now," he said.

"I beg your pardon?" said the Blustery Sergeant Major as if he hadn't heard correctly.

"I said," said Perseus, "it's up to us now."

"What's up to us now?" asked the Sergeant Major.

The Bugle Boy looked at the Sergeant Major as if he could not believe his ears. "What do you mean, 'What's up to us now?' " he asked defiantly.

For his part, the Sergeant Major looked down at the Bugle Boy as if he could not believe *his* ears. "What do you mean, what do I mean, 'What's up to us now?' "

Perseus looked at them both as if he could not believe *anyone's* ears. "He means," he said to the Sergeant Major, " 'What do you mean, what's up—' "

"I know perfectly well what he means!" snorted the Sergeant Major. "I mean, what does he mean by asking me what do I mean?" The Sergeant Major was now thoroughly confused as to what he meant. "What I mean is . . . *nothing* is up to us!"

"How can you say that?" Perseus demanded.

"Like this," said the Sergeant Major. "*Nothing* is up to us."

"But who's going to rescue Robin and Chingachgook and Princess Helen?" asked the Bugle Boy.

"That's not our concern," said the Sergeant Major. "Our job is to stay with the plane. Those are our orders and it's up to us to carry them out. As far as a rescue operation is concerned, that's a matter for reinforcements."

"But we have no reinforcements!" exclaimed Perseus.

"Then," said the Sergeant Major, "we have no duty to carry out any further actions and I am quite confident that any later inquiry will clearly show that we were in no way responsible for the disaster that's about to take place."

"Now listen to me," said Perseus. "If we don't do something to save our friends we won't have to worry about anything else because we won't exist!"

"We won't exist," muttered the Blustery Sergeant Major to himself.

"No," said Perseus, "we won't."

"And the Little Boy won't, either," said the Bugle Boy.

For the Bugle Boy, it was not simply a matter of not existing. The Little Boy was his friend and needed their help to find Davin.

"But," said the Blustery Sergeant Major, "I . . . I . . . I'm afraid."

Perseus and the Bugle Boy looked at him.

"It's all right to be afraid," said Perseus. "I'm afraid, too. It's just not all right to sit here and do nothing *because* we're afraid."

23

Escape—Part II

The plan was a desperate one but they had absolutely no other choice. The Bugle Boy sat in the rear cockpit of the dragon-winged biplane while Perseus got on one side of the propeller and the Sergeant Major got on the other.

"Heave!" whispered the Sergeant Major.

"Ho!" Perseus whispered back to him.

The Sergeant Major pushed against the propeller.

Perseus pulled against the propeller.

The Little Bugle Boy shoved the lever forward after each revolution and then when Perseus and the Sergeant Major had caught their breaths and were in position, he pulled the lever back and they heaved and ho'ed, pulled and pushed against the propeller, turning it round and round, winding the rubber-band motor ever tighter and tighter. Finally they had turned it as far as it would go and the Little Bugle Boy had shoved the lever forward, locking the propeller down.

Then the Sergeant Major climbed into the rear cockpit in front of the Bugle Boy.

"You're going to have to fly this thing, you know," the Bugle Boy said. "My feet won't reach the pedals."

"Try," said the Sergeant Major.

"I tried already," the Bugle Boy answered.

"Well, try again and stretch your toes!" said the Sergeant Major.

"It's no use," the Bugle Boy said, "my legs are too short."

"Drat!" said the Sergeant Major. "Drat and double drat."

Then Perseus climbed up onto the wing of the biplane and took a firm grip on one of the struts. "Contact!" he said.

"Contact," said the Bugle Boy, and he pulled back on the lever and the propeller began to spin furiously.

"Wwwwwhhhhhhhooooooooaaaaaaahhhhhh!" said the Sergeant Major as the plane taxied forward and plummeted off the edge of the shelf.

The Dark Knight nudged Princess Helen forward on the gangplank with his sword point. "Now, Your Highness," he said, "you will tell me where Davin is, or I'll signal my friend Blackbeard there to chop through that rope and send your friends to their deaths."

Princess Helen looked down. Blackbeard had raised his sword high above his head, ready to swing it down into

the fraying rope that was the only thing keeping Robin,
Chingachgook and El Lobo alive.

She said nothing.

"If you still will not talk," said the Dark Knight, "you
shall follow them to your own death. Ha ha ha ha ha ha
ha . . . ," he laughed.

Dangling from the rope, El Lobo heard the Dark
Knight laughing and said, "Ju know, I could be wrong
. . . but I do not think that that ees so funny."

A very strange sound filled the attic and grew louder. It
was the puckapuckapuckapuckapucka noise of a propeller
whirling through the air, and just over that noise there
was a terrifying bansheelike call that sounded something like this: Wwwwwwwhhhhhhhhhoooooooooooooo-
aaaaaaaaahhhhhhhhhhh!

"Down!" shouted the Little Bugle Boy into the Sergeant Major's ear.

"Which way is down?" called the Sergeant Major, who
could no longer see anything since he had covered his eyes
with his hands.

The Little Bugle Boy evidently did not think much of
that flying technique because he reached forward and
pulled the Sergeant Major's hands down off his eyes.

"Wwwwwwwwwhhhhhhhhhhoooooooooooooaaaaaaaaaa-
ahhhhh!" the Sergeant Major wailed even more loudly.

"Down down down down down down!" the Little Bugle Boy shouted, smacking the back of the Sergeant Major's head with every word.

The Sergeant Major barrel-rolled the aircraft into a

steep bank and put the dragon-winged biplane into a nosedive, heading straight toward the Dark Knight and Princess Helen.

Perseus held tight to the strut and began lowering himself from the wing like a circus acrobat. The Sergeant Major swooped the plane toward the Pirate Ship. Perseus hung low off the wheels, dangling from the plane with one hand, his other arm outstretched.

The Dark Knight saw the plane too late, and as the plane buzzed down, diving toward the gangplank, Perseus reached out his arm, swooped Princess Helen up off the gangplank and held her tightly as the plane veered away from the Pirate Ship.

"Shoot them down!" commanded the Dark Knight, standing alone on the gangplank, his sword pointing to where Princess Helen had just stood.

Blunderbusses belched smoke and cannons roared as lead filled the air, narrowly missing the dragon-winged plane.

"Oh dear," said the Sergeant Major, "oh dear, oh dear, oh dear, oh dear . . ."

Perseus held Princess Helen tightly. He had never seen a more beautiful creature in all his life.

"Uh . . . hi," he said awkwardly.

"Hi," said Princess Helen, who thought Perseus was easily the handsomest and most heroic figure she had ever met.

The Dark Knight's thoughts went in an entirely different direction.

"Kill them!" he bellowed at Blackbeard.

The cruel Pirate needed no encouragement. Without a moment's hesitation he swung down with his sword and cut through the rope that held Robin, Chingachgook and El Lobo.

"Wwwwwwwhhhhhhhhhhooooooooaaaaaaaaahhhh!" yelled Robin, Chingachgook and El Lobo as they plunged.

"Whhhhhhoooooooaaaaaahhhhh!" yelled the Blustery Sergeant Major as the Little Bugle Boy pushed him forward, causing the Sergeant Major to bank the plane ever more steeply into a desperate nosedive that looped the loop. The plane dove underneath Robin, Chingachgook and El Lobo, catching them squarely on top of the forward cockpit and saving them from their fall. The three rescued heroes clung to the plane with all their might.

"Good show, old man," said Robin to the Sergeant Major. "It was getting a bit sticky up there."

The Sergeant Major pulled back on the stick and the plane nosed up out of its deadly dive and leveled off. From up above, the cannons roared off the Pirate Ship's starboard bow, but they were too far out of range to do any harm to the plane and its occupants.

As he was preparing to land, the Sergeant Major saw her.

The Nanny's tabby cat.

Suddenly he was no longer afraid. Suddenly *he* had the power.

"H-e-r-e . . . puss puss puss . . . ," he said.

Nnnnnneeeeeeooooooowwwwwww . . . He swooped the plane down, aiming straight for the terrified cat, whose fur stood up straight and back arched high and tail fluffed out as she screeched like a Halloween witch. The Sergeant Major proceeded to dive-bomb toward her.

She jumped!

She ran!

She skedaddled as fast as any cat has ever skedaddled, straight across the attic floor, leaping through the attic door and out of sight. The Sergeant Major cried, "Take that, you villainous cat!"

The rubber-band engine sputtered and sputtered and finally stopped, and the dragon-winged biplane glided down to the attic floor.

"By Jove!" shouted the Sergeant Major. "It feels wonderful not to be afraid!"

Princess Helen and Perseus lowered the landing gear at the last moment and the plane skidded to a stop.

The Dark Knight watched from high above. "How amusing," he said to himself.

"Aaaaaaarrrrrh. They've escaped!" sneered Blackbeard the Pirate.

"Not at all," said the Dark Knight. "They will simply accomplish what we could never have done. The girl would not have talked. Now she doesn't have to. Now she and those other fools will lead us right to Davin!"

24

Harold

They were all a good deal shaken up. Robin, Chingachgook and El Lobo had bumps and bruises and aches and pains, especially El Lobo. His knees hurt, he had a back spasm and his elbow was giving him a bit of trouble as well.

"Are you all right, old chap?" Robin asked the Spaniard.

"One learns to lick his wounds only when the battle is over, *señor*."

"Yuck," said Chingachgook. "Why would anyone want to lick his wounds before, after or during a battle?"

"It was only a figure of speech, *señor*," said El Lobo, limping noticeably as he hopped down from the plane.

As for the Sergeant Major and the Bugle Boy, both of them were still excited about their recent adventure, especially the Sergeant Major. He banked his hands this way and that way, showing how he had flown the plane.

"Did you see the way that wretched cat ran?" he asked the Bugle Boy. "Not quite as brave anymore, I shouldn't think. Not quite as brave at all."

The Sergeant Major told it again from start to finish from the time he had taken off in the plane through the rescue and the escape and into the dive-bombing of his mortal enemy, the tabby cat. He relived his time of glory again.

"So here was the cat, you see?" he said. "And then here I come, streaking down out of the sun into the very jaws of death. Frightened, you ask? Frightened? Ha! I don't know the meaning of the word."

"It means afraid," said the Little Bugle Boy.

As for Princess Helen and Perseus, they said very little, only spent a great deal of time looking into one another's eyes.

"Pardon me," said El Lobo to them both.

"Huh?" said Perseus.

"What?" said Princess Helen.

"I said," said El Lobo, "I hate to interrupt but if ju had not noticed, we are not just out here to take a nice stroll together."

"We're not?" asked Perseus. "I mean, we're not," he said definitely. "No, of course not."

"No, of course not," said the old Spaniard, smiling. Then he put his arm around Perseus's shoulder and said, "Someday, my young friend, remind me to tell

you the story of when I was young and in love with
Maria Consuela and my heart was seared by the fiery
flames of passion. But for now, there is some business
at hand, no?"

He looked at Princess Helen and she flushed red with
embarrassment and said, "Yes, of course."

You see, they each knew only a part of the puzzle. It
was as if a map had been torn in two and each of them
possessed one half of it. Princess Helen knew that Davin
lived in a cave beneath the shadow of the Devil. The
problem was, she had no idea what that meant.

"Well," said Robin, "bears *do* live in caves."

"The problem is," said Chingachgook, "where do we
find a cave in an attic? Let alone a Devil or his shadow."

"The legends I have heard," said El Lobo, "say that it is
an overturned cardboard box."

The Sergeant Major peered into the darkness at the
stacks and stacks of cardboard boxes that seemed to fill
every corner of the attic. "Yes," he said. "Unfortunately,
there seem to be quite a number of those."

"In the shadow of *El Diablo*," said the aged masked
man.

El Lobo stopped and spoke in low, hushed tones, as if
he was afraid that some supernatural power could over-
hear him. "The Princess is right," he said. "The home of
the great and legendary Davin is said to be within the
shadow of *El Diablo*—the Devil—and next to a golden
urn. But where this is, I, too, do not know."

The Blustery Sergeant Major was harrumphing to himself when suddenly there was a flash of lightning that lit up the nighttime sky.

At least they thought it was lightning at first, but then when the attic shook violently they realized it was a bomb blast from the other war, the one that was going on outside. At any rate, there was a flash of light behind the statue of the gargoyle that cast its shadow through the skylight across the attic floor.

"Look!" said El Lobo, pointing at the gargoyle's shadow. "The shadow of *El Diablo*!" he said.

Sure enough, the shadow of the gargoyle stretched out toward the opposite wall, right up to what looked like a jungle of cardboard boxes. And there, peeking out from behind one of those selfsame boxes, was the handle of a gold-plated loving cup, a trophy from some bygone sporting event.

"The golden urn," said Princess Helen in awe.

A wave of excitement sped through each of them as they realized that the legends were true, that there indeed, in the shadow of the gargoyle next to a golden urn, was an upturned cardboard box that promised to be the secret cave in which they would find the great Davin.

"Well," said Robin, "what are we waiting for? Let's go, eh?"

"There is one thing more," El Lobo said gravely in a warning voice as he reached out and took Robin's arm to stop him.

"Yes?" Robin said. "And what's that?"

El Lobo looked each one of them straight in their eyes

to make sure they understood the full importance of his words. "The legends also say," he whispered, "that the great Davin is not alone."

"Not alone?" asked Chingachgook.

"Not alone," repeated El Lobo. "The legends say that he is protected, guarded night and day by a fierce . . . fire-breathing . . . dragon!"

There was a silence and then the Sergeant Major said, "Well, yes, but that's just . . . just a legend! That's all, just a legend."

"The whole thing is just a legend," said El Lobo, "but so far the legend has been true."

Slowly, cautiously, carefully, step by step, Robin, Chingachgook, El Lobo, the Little Bugle Boy and the Sergeant Major, Princess Helen and Perseus made their way through the shadows, across the attic floor, drawing closer and closer to the cardboard boxes. The closer they got, the bigger the boxes appeared, towering over them like cliffs and boulders. The passageways between the boxes became like narrow canyons leading this way and that, in a kind of maze, until they approached the golden urn and realized they must be nearing their objective.

"It must be around here someplace," Robin said, more to himself than to anyone else.

They heard a sound unlike anything they had ever heard. It was a metallic sound of metal clanking on metal and yet it was somehow alive, as if some gigantic iron creature, creaking and clanking as it walked, was coming closer and closer to them out of the darkness. It clanked and crunched and creaked its way nearer and nearer. The tiny band of adventurers huddled together in fear as another flash of light lit the nighttime sky and threw, for an instant, a giant shadow across their path . . . the shadow of a giant ferocious-looking dragon!

Robin and Chingachgook nocked their arrows, Perseus and El Lobo drew their swords, and around the corner into their cardboard canyon the shadow of the dragon loomed over them all. The clanking of the metal was deafening now, and when he appeared he was everything the legends had described, a gigantic iron monster.

His scales were made of metal, his rusty jaws creaked as his mouth opened wide and his huge head reared back. His tail thrashed about. He had giant steel fangs and made a grinding roar as his neck flew back and the dragon's head reared to belch forth the white-hot fire of a fire-breathing dragon.

The tiny band of heroes held on to one another in terror as the dragon's head leaned down toward them and he roared a mighty roar . . . and just as they expected fire to blaze out and cook them like a handful of marsh-mallows at a campfire, the dragon coughed a wheezing cough and made the sound of a punctured balloon, hacking out its last gasp of air before falling flat to the ground like a worn-out rag.

"Beheeeeehhhhhhhhhhhhhhhhhh . . . ," was the sound the poor old dragon made as he coughed again. "Beheeeeehhhhhhhhhhhhhhhhhh . . . ," he wheezed like a broken bagpipe.

The dragon was a very old dragon and the ferocious roar had taken quite a lot out of him, leaving him too worn to breathe fire.

"Beheeeeehhhhhhhhhhhhhhhh . . . ," he wheezed again, and said, "I beg your pardon . . . asthma, you see . . . Beheeeeehhhhhhhhhhhhhhhh . . ."

His name was Harold and he hadn't breathed fire in years. Like Davin, he had once belonged to the Little Boy's father, and now, long forgotten, he watched faithfully over his old friend.

The troop of heroes told Harold why they had come and that the Little Boy was dying. They told him that they had no hope unless the great Davin could help.

"Oh dear," said Harold, the rusty dragon, "oh dear." He shook his head slowly and it creaked awfully.

"You wouldn't have a spot of oil?" he asked hopefully.

"Terribly sorry," said Robin.

"Oh bother," said the old toy dragon. "A bit of oil would have been delightful. Well, I'd like to help, of course . . . wish I could, don'tcha know . . . but eh . . ."

"But eh what?" said the Little Bugle Boy. "We have to see Davin or the Little Boy will die."

"Yes, yes, quite so," Harold said, "but that's just the problem then, isn't it?"

"What?" demanded the Bugle Boy, who was thinking only of his friend and how much he needed Davin's help.

"It's Davin, you see," Harold said.

"What about him?"

"Well," said Harold, "he's rather ill himself, you see. Heart problem."

"He has a heart problem?" asked Perseus.

The old toy dragon nodded his head slowly and painfully. "Yes," he said, "it's broken, I'm afraid." He creaked as he nodded. "Has a broken heart, poor Davin, among other things, and then of course he's not altogether with-it anymore . . . bit senile, I'm afraid."

"Please," said the Bugle Boy. "We have no one else to turn to."

There was something about the Little Bugle Boy, how heartfelt his pleading had become and how obvious it was that he loved the Little Boy, that touched the old windup dragon's metal heart.

"Very well," he said. "I shouldn't get my hopes up if I were you."

"But hope is all we have," said the Little Bugle Boy.

And so, slowly, they made their way into the upturned cardboard box that formed the cavelike entrance to the lair of the great Davin.

◆ ◆ ◆ ◆ 25 ◆ ◆ ◆ ◆

Davin

It was very dark inside the musty old cardboard box and as they stepped into the darkness they heard a soft snoring sound, the sound of an old bear in deep deep hibernation, the sound of an old bear softly breathing in and out, sometimes snoring, sometimes making an almost painful sighing sound.

"There he is," said Harold, almost reverently, though his voice was full of affection for his old friend.

The eyes of Robin and Chingachgook, El Lobo and Perseus, Princess Helen and the Blustery Sergeant Major, and the Little Bugle Boy adjusted to the dark, and there in Davin's cave they saw him. He sat upright, leaning back in a corner, a very old teddy bear. His color was golden brown but there were many spots where the fur had been rubbed smooth by thousands of huggings. There were stains from tears and peanut butter. There were little tufts of stuffing protruding here and there and many places where Davin had been sewn and sewn and resewn to patch him up after all his wear and tear. One eye was stitched slightly higher than the other and the stitches just above his nose were frayed. His paws showed golden brown beneath the black that had been rubbed away. He had a soft fat belly and four plump legs and even though he slept, he looked somehow as if he were smiling. He looked to the Little Bugle Boy altogether huggable. He looked, in fact, like the most beautiful teddy bear anyone had ever seen.

"Ahem," said Harold, clearing his throat softly, hoping the sound would gently wake his friend.

The chubby old teddy bear sighed, however, and made a sound that sounded like Hummnahummnahummnahummna. He cozied back up in his corner and slept more deeply still.

"Ahem," Harold said more loudly this time, "ahem ahem."

Davin stirred without waking and smacked his lips softly and said in a low, rumbly voice like a papa lion purring, "Mmmmmmmm . . . stop ahemming, Harold."

The Little Bugle Boy poked the old toy dragon and urged him forward. Harold took a clanking step and then another, clanking up toward the sleeping teddy bear.

"Davin . . . ," he said, "I say, Davin . . . there's someone here."

Slowly the great Davin opened first one eye and then

the other and looked about him. When he spoke his voice
was lower still, a low and rumbly growl that vibrated in
the floorboards beneath their feet.

"Who," he said in the softest, warmest voice, "who is it
that's here and what do they want?"

Harold pushed the Little Bugle Boy forward with his
tail and nodded at him. "Speak, little one," he said.
"Don't be afraid."

The Little Bugle Boy took a deep breath and let it out
and then said in a squeaky little voice, "It's the Little Boy,
sir . . . we've been sent by the Little Boy, he . . . he's
sick, you see . . . burning up with the fever, that's what
the Doctor said . . . and he believes that you're the only
one who can make him well."

The great Davin leaned toward the Bugle Boy, his old
eyes growing clearer as he looked from the Bugle Boy to
Harold and back again.

"The Little Boy?" Davin said in his deep bass growly
voice. "The Little Boy?"

"Yes, sir," came the high-pitched squeaky reply.

Davin roused himself for the first time, suddenly full of
energy. He turned to Harold the dragon with growing
excitement and said, "You see, Harold . . . he didn't
forget me . . . he didn't forget old Davin after all! The
poor little fellow needs me? Of course I'll come. Up!" he
bellowed. "Get me up! Davin's going to make him well
again!"

It was obvious that the old bear had misunderstood.
When he had heard that the Little Boy was sick and

needed him, he'd thought it was the Little Boy's father. He thought it was long ago and the Little Boy's father and he were both still young.

"Davin," said Harold softly.

"What?" said Davin, and his voice rumbled more strongly. "What are we waiting for?"

"Davin," Harold said, "the, uh . . . the Little Boy he's speaking of is not . . . is not the same Little Boy that you remember."

Davin looked at him as if it were Harold who was senile. "What are you talking about?" he asked the dragon.

Harold cleared his throat and said, "That boy . . . grew up to be a man. He's an adult now, Davin, and has a son himself."

Davin's eyes narrowed suspiciously as he looked from one to the other, and then finally he said, "How long . . . have I been asleep, Harold . . . how long?"

Harold shuffled his metal feet and his scales creaked softly and he said in a very embarrassed way, "Oh . . . you know . . . twenty . . . perhaps twenty-five years . . . give or take."

"Twenty . . . five . . . years," said Davin softly. He sat back down against the cardboard wall of his sad and lonely cave. "Twenty-five years," he repeated, and shook his head slowly back and forth. The old bear's eyes grew misty and he let out a heartbreaking sigh as he said so softly that they could barely hear him, "Then he *did* forget about me . . . after all."

There was no sound there in the old bear's den except his labored breathing. All were silent. Finally Davin turned and looked up at the rusting metal dragon and said, "I'm very tired, Harold . . . I'm going back to sleep. Please don't wake me . . . ever again." And with that he slumped against the wall.

"No!" shouted the Little Bugle Boy, tugging at Davin's fur, trying desperately to pull him up. "You *can't* do that! If you don't come, the Little Boy will die. The Little Boy you remember was your friend. This Little Boy is *my* friend. You *have* to help him, please, oh please!" he cried.

"I'm afraid," said Harold, "it's no use. Nothing is as stubborn as a bear, especially this one."

But just then Davin opened one eye and looked at the Little Bugle Boy and said in his gravelly voice, "How does this friend of yours . . . know about me? I don't know about him . . . how does he know about me?"

No one dared breathe a word except the Little Bugle Boy, who stammered and said, "Well, I . . . I don't know. I suppose . . . I suppose his father must have told him about you . . . about when he was a little boy and his best friend in all the world was a teddy bear . . . named Davin."

Davin opened both eyes and looked at Harold and got up slowly and powerfully onto his haunches as if pulled out of his slumber by some force stronger than himself.

"You hear that, Harold?" he rumbled at his friend. "You hear?" he said, his voice growing stronger still. "The

Little Boy heard about me from his father! He *didn't* forget about me! Up! Harold, get . . . me . . . up!"

It was as if Davin were a young teddy bear once again. Harold, Robin and Chingachgook helped him up onto all four paws.

"Told him about Davin, did he?" Davin growled happily. "He should have given me to his little boy years ago, that's what he should've done, then old Davin could have kept him well, but still . . . better late than never!"

"Then you'll come with us?" asked the Bugle Boy as if he couldn't believe his ears.

"Come with you?" growled Davin. "Of course I'll come with you! The little fellow *needs* me! Let's go!"

So with Robin and Chingachgook and El Lobo helping on one side and Perseus, Princess Helen and the Bugle Boy on the other, and with Harold leading the way, the great Davin got to his feet and moved for the first time in twenty-five years to the opening of the cardboard cave that was his home.

As they came out of Davin's lair, though, their hearts sank. Arrayed before them and smiling cruelly were Blackbeard and the Dark Knight and all their evil minions.

"Thank you, Your Highness," sneered the Dark Knight. "We could never have found his hiding place without you."

26

The Final Battle

They were doomed. Perseus and Princess Helen knew it and so did El Lobo. Robin knew it, as did Chingachgook. The Blustery Sergeant Major did not know it, but he was afraid that it was the case. There was no way they could fight back, there was no way they could escape, there was no one who could rescue them. The Little Bugle Boy saw it in all his friends' faces and knew that their quest had ended and the forces of evil would triumph over all that was good. The only one who did not know how utterly and completely hopeless their situation had become was Davin.

It was not that he was a fool, for Davin, as everyone knew, was the wisest creature any child had ever believed in. It was not that he did not know who Blackbeard the Pirate and the Dark Knight were. They were evil and he recognized their faces and knew them only too well. No,

Davin did not accept the hopelessness of their situation because he knew one thing the others did not. He knew they had a secret weapon.

So while the others banded together in terror and readied themselves for the final battle, in which they knew in their heart of hearts they would be defeated, Davin turned to his oldest and dearest friend, Harold, with the utmost confidence.

"Harold," he said, in his wonderful low growly rumbly voice. "Fire!"

Harold looked at Davin without a trace of the confidence that the teddy bear seemed to have in such abundance.

"Beg pardon?" he said.

"I said," growled Davin, "fire!"

And so saying, he pointed with his paw at the Dark Knight and Blackbeard the Pirate and all their men, indicating that *they* were to be the targets of Harold the fire-breathing dragon's fiery breath.

"Oh yes," mumbled Harold, shuffling his metal feet, his scales clanking and creaking as he shifted his weight in embarrassment. "Fire, yes, of course," he muttered. "Yes, well, and then there's the problem . . . isn't it? I um . . . ahem . . ." He cleared his throat. "I, um . . . I'm not able to, actually."

He leaned down toward Davin and whispered confidentially, "No fire in the belly, you see . . . Haven't been able to cough up so much as a puff of smoke in years, I'm afraid."

The Little Bugle Boy looked from Harold to Davin. For a moment he had thought that perhaps there was a way out after all. Now it seemed his hopes were about to be dashed. But Davin did not hesitate for an instant.

He turned to Perseus and said in a low growling whisper, "You . . . boy . . ."

Perseus looked up at the bear.

Davin leaned ever so slightly toward the young hero, looking straight into his eyes. "Reach into my side," he said. "Pull out my stuffing . . . and stoke the dragon up."

Perseus did as he was told. There was a tear in the teddy bear's side, into which he reached his hand. He pulled out a handful of stuffing and looked questioningly at Harold.

There was a hatch in Harold's breastplate like a furnace door. Perseus opened it and stuck in the stuffing and suddenly Harold's eyes seemed to grow brighter and almost immediately there was a warmth that Perseus could feel near his hand and then just a wisp of gray smoke.

Harold looked down in surprise as well and turned to Perseus and whispered, "More . . ."

The Dark Knight's men advanced toward them. Davin turned to Perseus and whispered yet again, with more urgency in his voice, "Reach into my side. Pull out my stuffing."

Perseus did as he was told. Handful by handful he pulled the straw and cotton stuffing from the bear, and handful by handful he stoked the flames, which grew stronger and stronger still in the belly of the metal beast.

Black smoke snorted from the dragon's nostrils. The scales on his chest began to glow red-hot. Harold stood taller than before, his head rearing back, his jaws opened as smoke billowed out from his mouth.

"More . . . ," he said, and this time it was not a whisper but a voice grown stronger into a roar. "More!" he shouted as the Pirate's men and evil warriors of the Dark Knight's armies drew closer.

But with each handful of stuffing that Perseus removed, Davin grew smaller and smaller, weaker and weaker. The once huge bear crumpled in upon himself as the flames inside Harold grew stronger. Perseus looked up at Harold and said in a worried voice, "I can't take much more out of him, there won't be anything left."

Harold tried to cough up flame but the fire inside needed to be stronger.

"More!" he roared.

Perseus turned from the dragon to Davin. The bear's skin hung in folds and when Davin spoke again, it was barely above a whisper. "Reach into my side . . . ," he said.

"Davin," said Perseus, close to tears now himself, "I can't . . . there won't be anything left of you."

The Dark Knight's men and the Pirates were almost upon them. Davin whispered yet again, "Reach into my side, boy . . . Pull out my stuffing . . . Reach into my side . . ."

There was no choice but to make the sacrifice. Perseus

reached into Davin's side and pulled the last bit of stuff-

reached into Davin's side and pulled the last bit of stuffing out of the great bear, and as he did, Davin sank to the floor, as though the life had left him, too.

"Now, boy! Now!" bellowed Harold.

Perseus burned his hands upon the dragon's chest as he threw the stuffing in and the flames leaped higher. And as Harold looked down at Davin, lying on the floor, the smoke belched out and then the fire and then the roar!

Harold's head reared back and shot forward. His jaws opened and flames spewed from his mouth, shooting out like a volcano in one mighty blast of fire. Perseus and Princess Helen, Robin and Chingachgook, El Lobo, the Blustery Sergeant Major and the Little Bugle Boy turned away, holding their arms up against their faces to protect them from the flames.

"Nnnnnoooooooooo!" screamed the Dark Knight in agony as he melted to the floor.

"Auuuuuuuuaaarrrrrrrrrrhhhhhhhh!" bellowed Blackbeard as he turned to charcoal dust.

The flame burst out upon the evil warriors, the Headless Horsemen and Blackbeard's Pirate crew. All were left smoldering, either molten lead and tin in puddles, or burned and blackened through and through.

Robin, Chingachgook and El Lobo picked up what was left of Davin on one side, while Perseus, Princess Helen, the Bugle Boy and the Sergeant Major lifted up his other paw. Davin was empty, barely alive. Quickly they carried him past the charred remains of the evil army that just a moment before had seemed so invincible. They raced across the attic floor with but one thought in all their minds: to save the Little Boy.

Something made the Little Bugle Boy glance back over his shoulder. Perhaps it was instinct, perhaps it was a feeling of impending doom, but whatever it was, it made him stop, turn and look back toward the skylight. As he did, there was another blast of light outside that lit the sky and the building and the stone gargoyle that sat on its roof.

The gargoyle's stone claws seemed to clutch at the brickwork, which began to crack beneath its nails, crumbling into red dust beneath its claws.

The gargoyle reared back on its haunches. The Little Bugle Boy watched as the burst of light grew stronger and the shock wave of the bomb blast hit, exploding the building and sending the gargoyle screeching, stone wings spread, eyes aflame and glowing. The monster fell through the skylight, screaming, shattering glass across the attic and swooping down upon them.

This was no Dark Knight, no Pirate—this was, as the Spaniard had been saying, *El Diablo*! The Devil, the Devil himself in the shape of a stone monster hurtling down toward them, to destroy them one and all.

But just then another brilliant beam of light flooded the attic as the door opened wide and the overhead light snapped on, ending the darkness and turning the gargoyle back to stone that shattered immediately in a million pieces across the attic floor.

In the doorway stood the Little Boy's father. He wore the uniform of a pilot in the R.A.F. He stood there with his hand on the light switch looking at the shattered sky-light, the shards of broken glass and shattered stone that had been the gargoyle from the building across the alley-way.

"What on earth?" he said as he surveyed the remains of the miniature war that had been fought and lost and won. He did not see Perseus or the Bugle Boy, Princess Helen or the Sergeant Major, the Spaniard, Robin Hood or Chingachgook, the last of the Mohicans, there at his feet. He saw something, though . . . something that looked somehow very familiar.

He knelt amid the rubble of stone and glass and picked up Davin . . . what was left of Davin.

"I've been looking for you, old friend," he said, and, surveying the damage in the attic, he added softly, "Looks like you've been in a war, too."

The worn old teddy bear hung limp in his hands as he fought back tears. "Well," he said, "there's a little boy downstairs who means everything to me, who believes you have the power to make him well." And then, he added in a whisper, "Pray God he's right."

The Little Boy's father walked through the darkened house, down the stairs across the landing and into the Little Boy's room. On the child's nightstand stood a glass

166 jar full of cotton. Slowly, lovingly, the father took the cotton and, through the old bear's side, restuffed Davin till he was whole and plump and thoroughly huggable once again. Then he set the teddy bear down next to his sleeping, fevered child . . . and prayed.

27

Morning

"It's a miracle!" said the Doctor to the Little Boy's mother. He felt the child's forehead. "A miracle, I tell you!" he said.

Davin had been shoved to the edge of the bed for the Doctor's examination. The Little Boy's father and mother waited expectantly while the Doctor poked here and there, took their son's temperature and listened to his heart. But they knew already that the child's fever had broken, their prayers had been answered and their Little Boy was well and out of danger once again.

The Nanny bustled about the room and muttered to herself that *she* had never thought the child was *that* sick to begin with.

"Mollycoddlers," she muttered. "That's the problem, mollycoddlers."

The Little Boy's parents said nothing, or perhaps they

didn't hear until the Nanny screeched aloud and said, "*What* . . . is this filthy thing . . . doing here?" and with that she picked up Davin. "Where," she said in disgust, "did this filthy thing come from?"

She picked Davin up gingerly by the ear as if afraid to be contaminated by whatever germs he carried. "Straight to the dustbin!" she exclaimed.

"No!" the Little Boy cried out in anguish.

"Well," said his mother reasonably, "it *does* look awfully dirty, after all, and I'm sure it's full of dust. That *couldn't* be healthy . . . ," she said, and looked to the Doctor.

"No indeed," said the Doctor, "the last thing the child needs is dust."

"Yes," said the Nanny haughtily, as if she were the Queen of Hearts. "One needn't be a doctor to see that," and she proceeded on her way to throw the teddy out.

"No, you can't do that!" the Little Boy cried out again. "Not after all Perseus and Harold and all the others did to save Davin."

"Harold?" said the Little Boy's mother. "Who on earth is Harold?"

"Harold the fire-breathing dragon!" said the Little Boy as if everyone ought to have known who that was.

And there *was* someone who knew exactly who that was.

"Harold?" said the Little Boy's father, bending down to his son. "How did you know I called my old windup dragon Harold? *I* had even forgotten his name."

The Little Boy's father was very close to his son now, close enough so that the boy could share a secret.

"Because Davin told me," he said, and as he said it, he reached out his hands and pointed to the teddy bear, and his father plucked the old bear from the Nanny's fingers. The Little Boy hugged Davin close and whispered to his father, "All night long he told me stories. Stories of when you were a little boy and you and he had adventures with Harold the fire-breathing dragon."

The Little Boy's father looked at his son in amazement and brushed the child's hair back from his forehead.

The Nanny, however, pounced upon this as an example of the harmful effects of the child's upbringing. "The *idea* . . . ," she gobbled in her turkey voice, "the very idea! That's exactly what I've been saying . . . too much fantasy! Too much make-believe and faaaaar too many stories! Thinking that an old rag like that can talk! The very idea!"

The Little Boy's father looked at the Nanny with a steely-eyed glare. "Davin *can* talk," he said.

"I *beg* your pardon," gobbled the Nanny.

"I said," said the Little Boy's father, "Davin . . . can . . . talk."

The Nanny looked at him in shock.

"And any Nanny who does not believe in talking bears has no place in this nursery. *You,* my good woman, may leave!"

"Well!" gasped the Nanny, and she stormed out of the room never to return.

Later the Little Boy's father went up to the attic to bring back Harold the dragon, the Blustery Sergeant Major, Perseus and Princess Helen, to bring back El Lobo and Robin and his pal Chingachgook . . . and most of all, the Little Bugle Boy, who loved the Little Boy as much as any toy has ever loved any child who believed that the toy was real. The Little Boy's father brought these heroes back to the nursery, where they would have many more adventures with his son. For the father now remembered that time when he had known well what *all* children know . . . that toys come alive when grown-ups are asleep.

Grandma Goddess looked up from the book and saw three sleepy-eyed children with hot chocolate mustaches cuddled in their jammies and blankies, bundled up warm and falling asleep. She kissed them each on the forehead and whispered secrets in their ears. "Good night, my sweet children," she said, and softly turned out the light. "Good night."